I0764647

THE
CITY THAT WAITS
TO DIE

THE
CITY THAT WAITS
TO DIE

By

JL Walters

ISBN 978-0-9848987-0-1

Chapter One

My mind raced in half-sleep the morning tremblers began. My brothers and I slept atop a pallet of comforters, comfortable to a backside more like slab granite than feather bed, on the chill hardwood floor. The counterpanes and quilts were an accumulation of our parent's married life. The result of frugal family's bequeathed bedding on special occasions, removed from the massive linen closet. Each layer a manifestation of the value of work and abundance of affordable textiles: spend money on warm fabric, not coal to burn.

My baby brothers ridiculously idolized me, little siblings inevitably idolizing the eldest. They surrounded me, deeply embarked upon slumber along either side of my cramped, sweating carcass. The abandoned wrought iron bed-frame, springs, mattress - thick like the choicest steak - topped with accumulated plush rugs rested, empty, inches away. It was too high for entrusting fraternal safety when younger princelings stubbornly insisted on sleeping with their eldest brother. Exhausted, the bedstead noiselessly beckoned me through endless night. Exhausted, I thought of Clarice, whose firm embrace I left scant twilight hours earlier.

Abigail, just a baby on that trembling morning, slept in the nursery directly above. She was a curious little bugger even then, a baby who rarely cried, content within the bounds of her own private musings within a house of malcontents. A deep sleeper within a house of insomniacs, a rarified soul it seemed even then, neither pleased nor displeased with the prospect of rambling about the earth.

My entrenched young brother's were the malcontents, perpetually launching counterattacks via elbows and knees like rocks and arrows flung continually against backside and groin to interrupt illusive sleep nearly as often as I managed its location. Without their tortured old brother looming between, they slept smooshed to one another like a drawer full of tarnished cutlery. On cold nights, relocated into one bed together, they alternated clutching the blankets while turning, leaving the other shivering in the cold, as the self-swaddled sizzled with sweat.

As one sleeping brother stealthily maneuvered the sprawling postage-stamp quilt from me, again, our entire home began shaking. Distant morning noises emanating from an avenue far below receded. The city was quiet as I hazily propped upon an elbow, rotating my head, listening. A prolonged silence, I still have the impression, hung eternally, although moments long.

Distant neighbors screamed as rug-covered floors beneath interrupted slumbering bedsteads suddenly rolled, resembling secluded cockleshells violently unattached from moorings. The little boys hollered, jumping upon me. The bedroom wall overlooking the street divided, disengaged, rapidly dislocated from the house. Windowpanes, sconces, bookshelves, fell away as a banana expeditiously peeled. Assaulting frigid water-spray swirled billowing plaster-dust. Disturbing hiss and stench of odorized natural gas blended with reeking wrenched redwood rafters.

As the house shook, our pallet slid through the plume of plaster dust toward the expansive cavity. Ceiling plaster pendulums, cracked and loosed, swung in joist-wide strips, exposing knob-and-tube ceramic wire posts recently invisible beneath skinny lath boards. Indiscriminate prison bars, exposed galvanized water pipes, bisected the opening. Every remaining pane of glass in the room's remaining window frames shattered above our waltzing pallet of blankets and pillows. Before they or I knew, I hollered, "come, come, come," grasped each boy by his hair and dragged him as I scrambled to the back wall of the toiling room. We watched in terror as the mass of blankets, shattered glass, and chunks of plaster poured off the end of the hardwood floor into the avenue far below. We heard the room's detritus and additional wall torn from below plummet in a rolling cacophony upon the not so distant sidewalk. Breath escaped my lungs. Little boys clambered, scratching onto me in the freezing spraying water and gritty debris. Atop the opening where missing wall recently connected to ceiling, the nursery above commenced emptying its contents in a cascade of infantile toys, burp rags, diapers, and baby clothes. The irretrievable wall's absence stretched from the ground floor to the top of the house, tearing into attic.

Little boys rapidly pried away, they burrowed beneath comforters filthy with dusty water atop my neglected stationary bed as I, in stocking feet, suspenders entangled around my knees, jumped into the massive fissure. In the opening I grabbed a secure-feeling plumb pipe, frigid and smooth, stretched my totality, arms extended, into the shower of debris. A hopeless attempt to save baby Abigail as red mahogany bassinet slid to edge of rubble and caught fragments of wall just above. Climbing onto a remaining shard of wall along the side, splinters be damned, I was just able to support, with fingertips, the tottering leg of Baby's tottering bedstead. I heard Abigail whimper, still asleep. Cooing remained softly in my ears as another trembler struck and tumbled free the rubble above. The wooden leg tipped from my grasp. Bedclothes toppled and creamy blankets lined in lace spilled onto the growing mountain of debris thirty distant feet below.

Chunks of plaster bounced while clotting dust stung and blinded my eyes. I flailed beneath spilling bassinette groping after something solid within tangled bedclothes, locating a stout little arm. The sound of the snap I felt beneath my fingers was lost amidst Abigail's startled uproar. Clutching her through agonizing indignant hollering, I scrambled hastily down from my dizzying perch. Screaming infant tucked against my chest I assisted little brother's, suddenly smaller, hasty clothes collection. I ignored the terrifying glimpse burning my memory of the adjacent neighbor's house, collapsing, barely visible under naked early morning twilight. Boys clutching crumpled trousers, baby latching tight the tip of my pinky finger, rubbing her bumpy tongue along my fingernail tip, we scurried down an undulating servant's staircase. Outside, I jettisoned with my wards off the downstairs sleeping porch, as tremblers continued colliding.

Assembled before the house along the avenue and park-side curb, we discovered servants and neighbors in nightgowns, dressing gowns, pajamas, some partially undressed. Quickly I ushered my brothers to a neighbor who hustled them into the center of the disheveled street. Another tremor washed around the city, paving stones buckled underfoot, our avenue rolled and roiled like small choppy swells across a once-calm bay.

Brother's safe, I surveyed adult faces for recognition of mother or father. Instead, I located Abigail's nursemaid, who spoke no English, in her nightgown and nightcap. She franticly sifted the mountain of rubble, stubbornly dodging falling plaster along the front of the house. She repeatedly turned the miniature bassinet upside-down vainly searching for Baby, now missing, left sleeping within her charge. I pulled at the tiny Gaelic woman, Maude Bairhin, by the soggy hem of her flannel nightdress.

I spoke slowly, in broken Irish, into her tear-streaked face, "She's okay Maude. She's here. I have her but I think I broke her arm when I grabbed her."

"Oh Thomas I can't believe you have her. I just knew she was here in this pile and I couldn't find her for nothing."

She gingerly removed the baby from my grasp, "Oh, look at her little arm. We'll have to set that. Where's Cook, she'll know what to do with Baby's broken arm."

Clutching Abigail close, she bustled off toward a growing tessellation of stout old women wearing nightcaps grouped together along the edge of the park across the avenue. The cooks of our neighborhood wore nearly identical heavy flannel nightgowns, shoulders covered with thick black sweaters, loosed long screws of thick dark hair escaping white nightcaps eschew.

I searched for mother. I began to run back into the house when down the hill we all saw, in the dim light of sunrise, and then heard, the roof of a building sink in, sending a cloud of dust into the air below.

Avenue of neighbors watched a fiery jet erupt from a fractured gas pipe light and exploded. The blast destroyed the house neighboring the collapsed roof. Suction of air and voracious plume pulled a nearby unsuspecting gentleman wearing a black bowler hat and black suit jacket over white nightgown avoiding spilled roof wreckage sprawling prostrate. The explosion catapulted the poor fellow violently across the avenue. Just before this surprising spectacle, I spotted mother, standing centered within the avenue. She stood arrested, petrified by horror.

"Of course she was out of the house," I whispered to

the sunrise.

A perpetual early riser, mother attended church, lighting candles for her mother's and father's souls, before every sunrise. Then round to Steak-n-Egger Butcher Shoppe, selecting juicy chops for Cook's breakfast preparations, thick round bones for supper's pottage.

Mothered attempted ignorance regarding the nearby spectacle, examined everyone atop the hill, examined spectacular distant wreckage, remained motionless. Mother counted. She maintaining order amidst chaotic lives, the childish chaos, through addition and subtraction. Mother located her three boys, but lost Abigail. Her terrified countenance reflected mine earlier springing into missing wall, diapers, and bassinette raining onto bushes and sidewalk below.

Where's Abigail?

Mother repeatedly wrung her shaking hands unthinkingly, wiping them across creased calico skirts.

Where's Abigail?

Mother peered about while approaching, scanning for evidence indicating the stolen existence of Abigail and a sniveling nursemaid.

Where's Abigail?

Mother conversed briefly, distractedly, passed distraught neighbors wearing nightgowns, squeezing hands, never slowing her rapid ascent.

Where's Abigail?

Our closest neighbor's house earlier trembled until reduced to settling rubble. I witnessed its expedited collapse as Abigail's bassinette toppled. Another home reduced to rubble along another once pristine avenue within a city suddenly engineered to rubble. Abigail slept upon Maude

Bairhin's diminutive chest. Dreaming infant whimpered, painfully, occasionally shuddering as the houses had. Regardless of earthquakes, sleep interrupted demands completion.

Mother dropped butcher bundles, walked rapidly toward young Maude Bairhin.

Here's Abigail.

She confirmed her family's safety. She confirmed her four-month-old little daughter's continued existence, shadowed by our bisected home. Little baby Abigail slept safely.

"Goodness gracious," mother worried, "What happened? What happened to everybody?"

Tears tumbled along her ruddy cheeks. She sobbed softly, gingerly extracting Abigail from Maude's clutching arms, nursemaid bawling again, into her motherly embrace. The little baby whelped, began crying again with renewed vigor.

"Explain what happened," mother eventually managed her voice again after inspecting Abigail's fractured limb, and baby calmed into familiar maternal warmth. "How shall I explain to the Spencer's old parents, the absence of Mister and Missus Spencer, and baby Edward Spencer. Their home has disappeared. Have the three Spencer's at home also disappeared? What happened to our friends?"

Mother searched the changing horizon, the silhouetted rubble of the Spencer's demolished residence still settling, still producing rancid dust. She sobbed heavily, inconsolably. Absent, I realized, were the swarms of birdsong emanating from nearby park usually audible every sunrise.

"I barely realized what was happening, while it was occurring. Remain with the little ones while I help locate the

Spencer's."

Running from safety centered along the avenue, I leaped upon mountains of brick, crumbled cement, and mortar. Splintered timbers ripped my trouser legs. Scrambling, distant and nearby fire bells surrounding the shaken city commenced violently tolling, cutting eerie adjacent destruction clatter with startling sanctioned distress. Pungent wreckage aroma and natural gas stink evolved into, at first barely detectable, overwhelming fresh fire odor. Panic escalated into terror in my stomach, realizing the fate awaiting neighborhoods engulfed by inferno. I swallowed uncomfortably, throat swollen, fearfully dehydrated.

Excavating splintered shake roof using lengthy shards wrenched from shattered supporting rafters, I located Edward Spencer's mournful cradle.

Motionless, taciturn, as no baby clutched even by deepest slumber ever was, I slowly sifted wreckage, pulled blankets away, to reveal Edward Spencer's motionless little body. Miniature hands with fine slender fingers tapering to tiniest paper-thin fingernails curled gently, grasping the spotless afghan knitted by the maternal grandmother. A family treasure, Missus Spencer transported it from Donegal over twenty years before. Edward's innocent countenance was peaceful. No obvious trauma evident, he smelled pleasant, clean and untainted, and faintly of blooming flowers.

I gathered him gently, supported lolling head. I grabbed every blanket, every heavy rug from the littered little cradle, and regained my leaden feet. Edward felt like a sleeping baby, snuggly, welcomingly warm and cozy. One to cuddle and comfort until long after older brothers fell asleep.

Extending one arm holding wadded bedding for

balance, I followed precarious pathways returning to the front of the Spencer's destroyed house. The expanding assembly of gathering neighbors, shocked and deeply startled, wailed like trapped animals. The sky, usually so deeply blue, so bright and colorful through every breathtaking dawn, began transforming to ominously bloody pinks streaked with sinister smears of extending gray. A horizon bringing torrential weather under different circumstances, this morning reflected mortality echoing across hills and shattered roofs. The glowing sky reflected individual death, reflected unthinkable communal, municipal destruction.

Before that fateful morning we were collected individuals, a community shared in common neighborhoods, common locations of recreation, and common sunsets watched by occasional uncommon lovers. We worked, played, and worshiped together. That horrible morning we shared death. We shared trauma, soon to share common burial.

My little brothers huddled like puppies with mother holding Abigail sitting upon the far granite curb across the cobblestone avenue. Neighbors gathered after they migrated past the destruction, recognizing each other as waiting companions. Companions discovering comfort staring together at the surrounding spectacle, accidentally grappled together within binding numbing circumstance.

Their crying silenced. Neighbors ceased speaking. Friends released each other's hands from reaffirming grasps. The waning sense of aloneness redoubled each person's solitude at the recognized senseless bundle in my arms. Every grown person's countenance crossed from dread of infant mortality, to ridiculously hopeful relief, and then advanced quickly, abruptly onto confirmed tragedy.

The lengthy register totaling the victims would enroll Edward Spencer, innocent baby boy, with vast numbers of others yet undiscovered. Another of hundreds gone. No longer with bright clear eyes, ready smile, and love of anything easily fit into his greedy little baby mouth.

Mother remained stationary, perched upon the gray curb. She leaned against her exhausted little boys, each leaning uncomfortably against the park's encircling dark wrought iron fence. She stood awkwardly, and then sat abruptly down again with dreadful recognition as I approached clutching the quiet baby. Mother collected herself, stood again, and gently transferred Abigail, sleeping once more, to the nursemaid's chest. Exactly as they exchanged Abigail, sleeping soundly, so many countless previous times. As recently as last night, after Abigail finally dozed upon Father's chest before leaving for his shift with the Fire Company. Laurence McCurren, father, remained at work. Mother expected no communication from him until later this day. Now anticipating his return to our disheveled family possibly as late as tomorrow evening.

Holding the lifeless infant confused my crowded instincts. Not through repulsion over meaningless tragedy, rather through distorted fleeting sensations coveting his peaceful repose. Edward Spencer's universe, memories of this world, remained intact. My universe continued to unravel.

Mother lifted comforters from my drooping shoulders. She held the little baby boy she adored for such a momentary time. Warmth dissipated, still he smelled clean, sweet, of lavender wash. Regaining her seat, Angela McCurren held the still body upon her matronly lap, across ample skirts. I handed her additional bedclothes shaken free of plaster chunks retrieved from the rubble of our house, she proceeded swaddling him the way all loving parents enwrap newborn babies. Her wrappings failed his inadvertent revival.

"Thomas McCurren," mother's voice cracked looking into my face shadowed by morning's glowing, darkening sky, "Where shall this infant be buried?"

Snow fell silently, distracting me, I nearly missed the quiet question.

"We keep him safe until Mister Spencer buries him. He will bury the baby with Missus Spencer soon as she's recovered."

Snow landed thicker, incredible anytime, dotting white flakes across our shoulders and disheveled hair. Snowfall anytime, accompanying an earthquake on an April morning nearly on Easter Sunday, was unfathomable.

Continual surreal circumstances that morning failed in eliciting surprise amongst exhausted neighbors wearing nightgowns. The multitude watched, silently, the snow's fall.

Tasting a heavy, awkward flake gently removed from my shirtsleeve, "Ash. Just listen to those bells."

The city was burning, and we smelled the inferno. The blazes explained why every distant vista appeared glowing. I thought sunrise was causing the glow but burning fires created the distracting diffusion of unearthly colors. The inadequate Fire Company would be overwhelmed.

As we watched the far city begin to smolder, a group of men on horseback rode up the hill from the west. They stumbled upon an arresting scene of devastation in the middle of the street. James Pritchard, City Council Representative, McCurren next-door neighbor, business partner, and close family friend, lead the group. He spotted Angela McCurren surrounded by her children and distraught, bedraggled neighbors. Our nightclothes and modestly gathered bed sheets did not surprise him. The entire district of Ashbury Heights was naked or clutching cloth to cover nakedness.

James jumped from his horse and walked over. Giving me a bracing hug he asked, "What is the situation here Thomas?"

"Mister Pritchard, sir, we are all of us okay, but it looks like too many are missing from our street for there to be much good news today." I added slowly, "No one has seen Mister and Missus Spencer. We found the baby. He's dead. Ma wants to know where we are to bury him."

"Mister Mann," James Pritchard called back to the group riding with him, "Set your team to sifting these houses, and send a runner after news of the fire. I want all survivors here relocated to the Avenue Drive. We'll need clean water before you know it. Start by draining any ponds or fountains you can think of into buckets and barrels before refugees ruin them.

"Send a man to the church and ask after Father August. Let him or anyone else you see there, if the building still stands, know we shall be sending the dead, and wounded to them. We'll want all the pews and God knows we'll need the father's holy services. If there were any sisters not at hospital when it collapsed have them make ready. The boys sifting the hospital wreckage will be at the church with all they find so move out, at a high step, now!"

Another boy started running, "Have them ring one bell five times if the building is still standing," James hollered after the lad as he sped away, barefoot, over the mounds of upturned paving stones and debris.

"Angela my dear, I am so very sorry for our

neighbors. I just left Laurence, he and his men are well but will be overwhelmed by the blazes soon enough. They are headed into the center of the city and the worst of the damage."

Mother nodded, fear and shock held her voice.

"Now boys," he called to more of the men on horseback, "I want a quick check of these houses. You know who lives in them so note who is missing and who survived, with detailed reports of damage above and below the street."

Men spurred mounts, boys ran behind. Up and down the street, they noted the damage and reported what they found to a clerk in a small wagon with portable desk, pen, and ink. More wagons arrived and men with huge wrenches and thick pry bars descended into manholes to turn off gas mains and inspect plumbing. Others ran into houses and opened windows after the leaks ceased, to air them out and avoid further explosions.

Another crew ran from house to house trailing the inspectors nailing doors and windows shut to prevent distraught owners from returning into dangerous dwellings and to prevent looting. The sudden activity awed the inactive, mourning citizens, as intended.

"My friends," James climbed onto the back of his clerk's wagon. He addressed his neighbors in a voice meant to comfort, calm, inform, "Our beloved Mayor Schmitz has given a shoot to kill order for looting. The police will follow it. So will the federal troops who are at this very moment mobilizing across our poor devastated city. We must make sure none of us is mistakenly shot. Be warned: Do not take any liberties."

"As to the wounded, our beautiful Saint Mary's

hospital was demolished in the quake: A complete loss. Instead, we will move our wounded into the Saint Mary's cathedral. Teams will be here shortly for that work. As to the dead, we will recover our dead as soon as we see to the living. We will move the dead we know of to the churchyard. The teams will take care of this for you too. We are setting up temporary quarters along the Avenue Drive for all our neighbors. This is where I need you to go as soon as you can. There will be food and clean water and less chance of injury due to further falling debris or additional tremblers."

We listened to James Pritchard with rapt attention. He was an angel sent to guide us through the sudden turmoil of lives turned upside down.

He stood six feet six inches tall. He not only towered over most other men, he dominated them. The one or two he could not dominate or reason with he punched in the throat while they were still talking. A trick learned from his very wise father. If his blow missed its target, he agreed to work with them. Mister Pritchard became the City Council Representative for his district by negotiating each of the other candidates out of the race.

After his first day at city hall, he told his pal Laurence, "Hell, I may end up Mayor of this city one day if I can muster enough diplomacy to accommodate the opposition."

He kept his black curly hair and moustache clean and well adorned. He wore staggeringly expensive light colored suits and hats, solid gold jewelry, fine linen shirts and silk ties. The parts of him not covered with the finest cloths shone brightly in all light. His wife, like his house, was tall, pale, and beautifully built for entertaining. Both did quite a bit of entertaining.

Abigail Pritchard and mother were schoolgirls and

friends their entire lives. The McCurrens named Baby Abby for Abigail Pritchard. Abigail Pritchard helped mother deliver each of her children. mother helped Abigail with the birth of her boy Donald.

"My dear," James spoke quietly to Angela while helping her to her feet, "I am sending you and the family across the bay. Most of the houses on our hill survived the quakes but may not survive the fires if they come this far. I won't see you and my Godson's in a refugee camp. We will do the best we can with tents and accommodations but they will in no way be up to snuff.

"You know Abigail, Donald, and Melinda are in Sausalito with Abigail's brother. I sent a boat over for supplies and to let her know I am safe. I'll send you to the pier and get you across to join them on the estate. I spoke to Laurence and he agreed this is the best thing for the children. It will give you and Abigail a chance to catch up. I need to keep Thom here with me. Laurence wants him here too."

She looked into his face for a moment, "We will go now. I do not want to be in this destruction. I do not want to witness the chaos sure to follow. I am all too familiar with the ways of men and women given to their own judgment and have no desire to sleep with a shotgun across my bedstead." Angela was a woman of precise words. Those who knew her listened when she spoke.

"I'll send word to Laurence you are safe. You'll take a wagon and one of my teamsters and a host of Pinkertons. We'll get all the things you need and send you and the children on your way to the pier to meet the boat's return."

Looking around, "Sounds like the boys have given the a-okay for Thom here to go into the house. Just stay away from that front wall if you can, all right son? Your Ma will rest a moment longer. Laurence sent a squad to soak the remaining structures on Buena Vista Avenue to thwart the fires. When the fires approach this hill will make a good lookout point for directing pump wagons."

She looked into his face. In it, she saw the death already witnessed this early morning. He misinterpreted her silence as acquiescence as he gently helped her into a wagon with the baby and two smaller boys. She grabbed at her skirts and an early morning shawl too thin for the wind that stirred up smoke, ash, and water from far away fires.

I returned with bundles of blankets full of the things we might need. I gave each a kiss and waved as the wagon slowly rumbled down the debris-laden street. It was a long wagon, large enough to carry the McCurrens and the things we needed away from the destruction around our house. The boys were excited to ride, mother reluctant to leave our beautiful home.

Chapter Two

At an intersection down the hill from their park, the little boys heard a clock cuckoo from beneath nearby rubble. Neighbors smartly restrained the clock's owner; they kept him from digging in the rubble. He hollered, "Josie's clock! Josie's clock!" Fat tears streamed down his red cheeks.

Preventing his plunge into the boards and bricks proved too difficult for his two friends, they beckoned others to help them save the anguished man from himself. With promises of salvage and four neighbors holding him, he was mollified.

When the McCurrens crossed the Avenue Drive, the boys no longer frolicked in the wagon. The tour of the neighborhood with so many of the houses and buildings that made the neighborhood their home missing, stunned and silenced momentarily misplaced wagon-ride joy.

"It's just fill for dumping into the bay now," the old teamster whose job it was to drive them to the pier sadly quipped with a tear on his cheek and thick tobacco juice dribbling down his chin.

All were shocked to find their world gone. Shocked further to find the people collected in tents and lines for food in a park usually reserved for summer romps and winter walks. They did not see all of the people they missed. Mothers with missing children lacked the look in their eye of a person connected to this world. Small children sat on dirty bottoms, faces marked with the terror of waking to find mothers and fathers suddenly gone. Ripped clothes had failed to hide the frailty of broken bodies hugged just the night before, making orphaned children quickly intimate with the form death takes. Relatives and neighbors worked to relieve the children's distress and sneak a little broth into small, grief-swollen bellies.

The Avenue Drive was dark with the smell of fire in the air. As on the street atop Buena Vista, ash accumulated and covered every surface. The men of the military sternly organized and transformed the park into a camp. Into a sea of white tents bisected by lines of citizens in black coats and dark trousers, neighbors waiting for food and clean water and the use of a legitimate latrine. Young and old quickly discovered fighting and mischief tolerated by a hard crack from a truncheon or a kick from a polished government-supplied boot.

Odor overwhelmed everyone. The sweet smell of lumber, the stink of wet plaster, the occasional heart racing scent of gas. The smells of destruction soon mixed with the odors of human closeness and those of swollen dead animals wet in the gutter. Death and rot mixed with acidic burning in eyes and throats. Ash and soot lined every surface. Black, oily trickles of water ran down every boulevard. Only the desperately thirsty or those mad with grief and sudden horror attempted to drink the water that washed the fires and the dead.

Downtown the inferno engulfed and raged. Squads of workers dynamited buildings to prevent the rapid spread of the devastation but not always successfully or safely. Teams of men worked with teams of horses to pull remaining walls and buildings down lest they fall on the unsuspecting salvage worker or one of the many souls who wandered the city. Everyone sifted piles of rubble. They dug for the dead with fingertips made bloody with torn nails and skin ripped on brick, mortar, and lethal shards of splintered redwood, spruce, fir, and pine. Police officers restrained the bold senseless ravings of the insanely grieving as best they could.

Officers assigned to neighborhood patrols fast became fearful, terrified watchers of the desperate. Lifelong friends and acquaintances made crazy and angry by grief and loss directed their rage at the men whose job it was, they supposed, to prevent such catastrophe. By their mere civic presence, peace was to have reigned supreme forever and always. Incredibly only one officer was reported missing. His family and brother officers recovered his broken body only after the cleanup crews cleared the ash and rubble away from his imperfect tomb. The piles of bricks that accidentally or maliciously covered his dead body also covered the body of a young girl. Some speculated over a lurid connection between the two. A convenient blanket of fallen brick could cover a third person's justice. No witnesses came forth. The officer's fraternal peers kept speculation to a low minimum.

"Our heroes will be remembered by God. We will rebuild our city in a manner befitting of the glory of the new century. San Francisco is the city of the Phoenix: She shall rise from the ashes stronger and better prepared for future tests be they by the cruel hand of nature or the sordid hand of man," Again James stood in the bed of a wagon. He addressed the collection of survivors gathered in the Avenue Drive.

Ash swirled. Winds blew hard from the west. James spoke with confidence because his family and the family of his best friend were safely across the bay or on their way across the bay. Their mansions on the hill were relatively undamaged. They were among the fortunate. "If my family was taken from me or my home destroyed," he thought, "These are words I would need to hear to keep me sane."

"Our hearts are one. Every daughter and son torn

from you is torn from us. We lost a part of ourselves, a part of our souls, in this tragedy. We will heal one another. We will heal together. We will heal and we shall be stronger."

He climbed from the wagon and embraced a few of the crying. He ruffled the hair of gawking lads. James shook the hands of broken men, one hand clasping their elbow or shoulder as he peered into their ruddy faces, the depth of his concern clear and serious for them to see and depend upon in their weakness.

He hid his tired mind, the lists of things, of people to work on. Already his wife Abigail and grown son Donald were coordinating barges of building materials and wagons by the score to remove debris and rebuild their neighborhood. Banking did not stop due to disaster, the Pritchards and McCurrens grasped enough advantage to ensure Ashbury Heights rebuilt before work crews cleared the destruction downtown.

James shook hands and offered consoling words until his driver took him by the arm and made his excuses to the crowd. Edgar Pepper was a snake of a man. He wore a bowler hat and a cheap black suit. His freckles and glasses made him look like a fat kid stuffed into a skinny man's body.

"The family has been removed to the yacht. As we speak, they are being sped to the house across the bay, should be in Sausalito long before nightfall." Edgar Pepper sucked his teeth before and after he spoke.

"That's good Edgar. We need to return to the top of Buena Vista immediately. I have a few details to check. Then we must locate Laurence McCurren and his father. We need ready cash; we need a lot of ready cash."

Edgar sucked and looked at the crowd, "None of us should have to spend one night in this city of hell." He sucked again and looked at James, "I don't know how you do it. My cheeks ache with all the damn looks of sympathy I've been giving the filthy and miserable. Only a day ago they held even less of my genuine interest. Amazing a bit of dusty misfortune and fire can reduce the voters to their basest selves," He sucked.

"Shut up Edgar. I don't need to hear your prattle now."

"Okay Mister Pritchard," Edgar sucked again. "I swear, in each old lady's care-worn face I only see naked, wild whores downtown. Skirts lifted, arms bare, sloppy breasts pressed against me."

"And I swear if you don't shut the hell up I'll throw you under these horses until one of them caves your head in." James tolerated Edgar because he was a useful snake. Time and stress clearly illuminated the nature of each man. In Edgar, it illuminated that he lacked the ability to rise above himself.

James stopped and sat on a bench. He bounced two crying babies on his knees. "My dear they are children, a bit of nose dirt will not hurt them or me. Tell me of the condition of your house." Their mother made a fuss over their snot-encrusted noses as he lifted them. As James spoke to the woman Edgar watched little yellow and green bubbles, blow and pop from baby nostrils on each exhalation. He felt his bowels turn thin with thoughts of impending typhoid and tuberculosis. A yacht and his escape from death could not come too quickly.

"Being his toady may be the death of me," Edgar thought, "But that death will come in clean sheets with unbound auburn fruit-and-flower-scented hair on a pillow next to me. James Pritchard is a fool." Edgar imagined the safe in the big house on the hill and the money in a dead James Pritchard's portmanteau pried from a stiffening grasp. He sucked his teeth.

"Unanticipated circumstances," Edgar sucked to himself, "facilitate unrealized ambitions."

James Pritchard learned many things from his father and his father's old partner Finney "First Punch" McCurren.

"Rich people," Finney McCurren said one bright summer's day,

"And poor people," Lucas Pritchard added,

"Spar with words, whenever they speak."

"Even if they sound like they're being amiable and conciliatory," The old man went on, "they ain't."

"It is the strange middle people, neither-rich-nor-poor, who are their mutual target, shared foe. No poor person can possibly injure a rich person with words. No rich person could possibly bother a poor person past irritation or inconvenience. The neither-rich-nor-poor are their common enemy,"

"Unsuspecting dupe."

"Neither-rich-nor-poor give their money and their votes,"

"And their daughters," Lucas added,

"And their daughters," Finney agreed, "to the rich in a hope of currying favor. The poor steal all these things when they can."

"Irony is, the neither-rich-nor-poor have no idea they are hated by all. They are the pawns of all. Really rich folk and really poor folk are disconnected from the trivial past-times of life."

"What the neither-rich-nor-poor don't understand is, barbed words from rotten or polished teeth alike are always meant to destroy one class of person: Them."

James Pritchard listened but did not believe the old men. They stood on the porch of one of the Buena Vista mansions scanning the view of the bay from the center of the city. Tobacco smoke swirled as they told their sons, Laurence and James, these truths and many others observed in two lifetimes of marauding, swindling, and heavy-handed financial manipulations.

After years in local politics, James saw for himself they were right. It was why his constituents loved him. He did not challenge or pander to them, he spent most of his time taking shots at himself and his peers. An activity everyone encouraged and enjoyed. James Pritchard's rule in politics was one Finney told them during a front porch tutorial.

"I was regularly acquainted with an old gap-toothed whore in my youth," Finney, it seemed, knew every whore in California at least once. "One night we were getting drunk after a bit of business and she said to me, "Finney, if you're a pleasin' 'em wit' one o' 'yer hands use t'other hand ta' please yer' se'f."

"By this of course she was sayin' steal their money while you have 'em distracted. At the time I figured she meant some kind of mutual sexual thing."

James Pritchard stole their hearts and their votes as he made them feel good with his self-deprecating words. Sincerity was his best trait and the most false he could perfectly project. So perfect a false projection his wife loathed his sincerity having long ago discovered the sincerity of his marital fidelity found itself at home between the thighs of the mothers, sisters, wives, and daughters of the district's voters.

Chapter Three

Abigail Pritchard's sincerity rested in her child and in herself. She indulged additional needs with a series of gardeners who pruned, nourished, and encouraged her to bloom through one season following another.

She easily bossed the gardeners around the garden, in the greenhouse and her bedroom. She easily fired them. She easily replaced them when they grew too bold. They always grew too bold. She tired of their inevitable familiarity and the way all men, even servants and hired laborers, eventually convinced themselves they really knew or owned a woman because she clenching their shoulders while she spasmed and panted hot on their neck as she bit their earlobe or the meat of her own sore thumb.

She knew James Pritchard's weaknesses. In the past, more often than not, she was glad to be free from his lusts.

"I once loved him," she poured another drink and lay on the veranda watching smoke rise across the bay. She kept an eye out for approaching private pleasure crafts. "Maybe I still do. Has it grown over the years or has it died? We are such a part of each other's separate lives I cannot tell. He introduced me to my own lusts and physical cravings. In recent years, his taste with others and me turned from an eagerness to please to a lazy demand to be pleased. Work is not something I am accustomed to performing. Neither as a child nor an adult, least of all in my own bedroom."

Abigail's lifelong friend Angela McCurren claimed to still lust after the only love she ever knew; her strapping husband Laurence. Laurence was a busy firefighter even before they married, so many years ago, and Abigail enjoyed the time she spent with Angela and the family. Being with them in Sausalito would be a wonderful distraction from the mayhem across the bay.

“I always hated city life,” Abigail thought brushing her long brown hair, “the odors, and the rudeness of strangers. The bustle increased, the last few years, to a point, in my opinion, where the city simply could not go on. A fire was,” she peered at the smoke rising into the clouds and blowing inland, “even as the result of an earthquake, inevitable. Too bad. It must have ruined so many fine homes and shops. At least it missed Easter. There were too many people in too cramped a space. The fire and the quake will see to a little thinning by God and Mother Nature.”

Many of the people whom she suspected survived, along with their houses and possessions, in her opinion deserved to survive.

“The righteous, who the poor and lazy live off, must survive. The hardworking, the inheritors of fortunes, have so much responsibility, even without the poor and lazy continually pandering for another handout and another way to avoid a full day's work. Now there will be fewer of them. Fewer to deal with. Fewer to look at on the streets in their cheap hats, depressing black suits and awful, sober dresses. Where did they all come from?”

She understood the need for Chinatown, to keep the oriental habits together and away from the original families.

“But what about those who look like normal people? Where did they come from? The ones who make all the buggy traffic and the long lines at the theatre and go to the park laughing so loudly, leaving chicken bones and bread crusts about the benches and public grounds? They are the ones who brought the rats and the lice and the diseases. They must be the worst of the worst. Why else would they leave their homes for my city? Why would they leave their families if they were the least bit wanted at home? They must be the dregs of wherever they came from. At least the Orientals built the railroad. Paid for their time and owed nothing further. The rest of them, however, do not want to work. Do not want to be clean. Do not want to contribute anything to the city, to their neighbors. They are foreign leeches sent here by their governments to weaken us from the inside out.

"God knows I have gone through more gardeners and grooms in the last year than any previous. Not one was good looking. Their dark hair and dark skin and large noses repulse me. Any attempt to understand what they are saying in their thick accents is a waste of time. Of course, they could not understand me either. Thank God, Cook is always at hand. She seems to have a way with the uneducated, the brutish. It is probably the food. They tolerate Cook more than they tolerate the lady of the house. They know Cook feeds them. Whom do they suppose bought the stove and the coal and gas and food Cook cooked? Whom do they suppose approves the menus each and every day? I suppose some of them were nice to look at. Those men who built the retaining wall were fine and sweaty and strong."

Closing her eyes, she smelled the musky scent. She saw their bare glistening backs streaked with mortar and mud. Strong hands and legs lifted the blocks to build the wall. She imagined they lifted her too. Their sweat dripped onto her bare chest.

"The old foreman became so nervous when I stood and watched them work," she told herself. "To keep him on edge I offered every harsh criticism with which I could come up. I was watching his men. Just one in particular, the brawny man with broad shoulders and thick legs. I imagined the taste of his sweaty skin in my mouth as I whimpered under the weight of his great chest. He is the one I will contract to rebuild anything in need of repair when we return to the city. His deep black hair and pale green eyes, I want him. Not a word will he understand from me. I will whisper all the nasty things I think of him and his people into and leave clenched bite marks upon the lobes of his small ears."

She opened her eyes and saw the yacht docking at the pier. She rose and finished her drink. She found a parasol, walked down the stairs, across the green to water's edge, and down the shore to the pier. Her friend and three children looked like visitors from another world. Their faces were sunken and pale. She noticed each of them was crying as the crew assisted them onto the wooden pier.

"Where is Thomas?" Abigail asked, "Oh my God. Angela where is Thomas?" Her voice cracked, eyes moistened. Angela took her in her arms as servants and the yacht's crew began unloading McCurren possessions onto the private pier.

"Thomas is fine."

Abigail was sobbing.

"Sweetie, I left him with James."

"The look on your face," Abigail continued sobbing, "Your dire countenance. I did not see Thomas. I honestly believed he was gone. Why are you so pale? What is wrong then?"

"The Spencers are missing. Are gone. Are dead. Thomas found the baby in his crib. The poor little thing. Thomas handed the poor baby to me. I honestly believed he was asleep. He grew cold and pale. Ashy like my father when we found he passed in the night, when I was a girl."

"I remember. What will they do? What will they do

without little Martin Spencer to smile at them? At us?"

"I do not think they are alive. I think they are better dead with the baby dead. They waited their entire lives for him. We left baby Martin with the Sisters at the church to be buried later, at the appropriate time."

Angela looked across the blue water to the dark sky above the ravaged city. "Now I will pray to die before any of ours are taken from me. Now I will pray to God that He spare me the grief of a mother."

"I will pray too. I will pray to be spared the grief of a mother too."

Chapter Four

I stayed behind; James paired me with his driver, Edgar Pepper. As we hopped into the funny little automobile, Edgar Pepper sucked his teeth.

"You know how to shoot a rifle?"

He sucked his teeth again.

"Yes sir," was my reply.

"Anyone tries to stop this automobile; I mean if anyone approaches us from either side or steps in front of us, you shoot them in the gut. If you aim for their belly you may hit something and scare off any others watching, waiting."

"Listen to Edgar Pepper here Thom; he used to drive for the governor. When Edgar, two terms ago?" James was able to tear himself from the Avenue Drive refugee camp. "I need to go to the house before we go to the pier, boys. I need to get there fast."

Edgar sucked his teeth, "last term."

James Pritchard and my father Laurence McCurren kept valuables and lists of useful information in a safe built into the wall of a closet on the fourth floor of our house. To access the safe a section of false wall, on pulleys, rose from the floor to the ceiling. When up, it revealed a section of wall with a few sidearm's, a few bladed weapons and the door of my grandfather Finney's large safe.

The door was brass and iron. The tumbler knob was as big as a teacup. The combination was a sequence of eight pairs of numbers with two complete turns of the knob between each pair. The safe was time consuming and difficult to open. A time lock added to the difficulty.

Edgar Pepper drove James Pritchard and me from the Avenue Drive to the houses on Buena Vista Avenue quickly, without disturbance. We stopped and parked in front between the tall mansions. Edgar and I escorted James across the front walk to the McCurren house. A fire sentry and a few Pinkertons stood in the front yard.

"Gentlemen, good to see you well. Any trouble this dark day?" James asked as he firmly shook each man's hand.

"No sir," the small pale fire sentry replied.

"There was one small blaze at the bottom of the other side of the hill. Bobby Watson took and lined up as many filled buckets as he was able to find around your and Lieutenant McCurren's houses. Just in case. Hope they won't be a needed today. Looks like the main fire ain't gonna spread much further west than the Van Ness line."

"Good, good. Let's hope not," James replied. "I will be staying across the bay tonight with my family. You all know where the kitchen and the beer in the cellar are; make yourselves comfortable. Just not too comfortable, understand."

Chuckles went all around.

"I trust your families and loved ones are as safe as we can make them. If not, let Mister Oliver or Mister Pepper know so they may direct more men to safeguard either them or your homes, as needed. Or help you make other arrangements as required. I have business inside and believe each of you always has further preparations to make or tasks to mind."

They nodded and resumed checking weapons and securing the many first floor windows of each house.

Quietly James took the fire sentry aside, "Has there been any change at the Spencer house? Any sign of them?"

The slight man touched the rim of his worn cap. In an afterthought removed it from his bald head and clutched it to his chest.

"Yes sir. We found both under a pile. Still on the bed. Both dead, sir. We're a fixin' to get them down to their baby at the church. The Sisters told us what to do and how to bring them down."

James breathed for a moment. The neighbors on top of Buena Vista were close. They shared in each other's unanticipated happiness, joy, sorrow, and regrets. Donald Spencer was James Pritchard and Laurence McCurren's boyhood friend. They grew up on Buena Vista together. James and Abigail named their son for Donald Spencer. He was their attorney for as long as business and life required legal advice and intervention. Louisa Spencer met Abigail and Angela as a young girl at finishing school. They supported Louisa through every painful step of trying to get pregnant and God knows how many miscarriages. Both assisted in the birth of baby Martin. Now they were gone.

James showed a brave face.

"That is a shame. I suppose it may be better though, spared the death of a baby. I hope none of us ever has to know for sure."

He paused again.

Motioning me to follow, James unlocked the front door and we entered. We crossed the front rooms, navigated to the rear of the house, and mounted the back stairs.

As we climbed the creaky boards, James checked his heavy gold watch, "We will finish here quickly. Then we will find Laurence and tell him your family is safely in Sausalito. No need to mention the Spencers. No good can come from distracting the heart of a man during the most difficult time of his, our, professional life.

"What are we doing in my house Mister Pritchard?" I

felt awkward skulking up the servant stairs pursuing an unknown task.

"You know how close our families are. We have been for decades. When your grandfather and my father built these houses they designed a Keep in yours, you know what a Keep is?"

"I do. It's a secluded safe place in a castle, like King Arthur?" I was poaching on unfamiliar property.

"Exactly."

James rounded each creaky landing heading to the fourth floor above.

"Our families share much. The most important things we share are secrets. I need to show you where we keep the secrets. Where we secret the history. Your father should be doing this but circumstance prevents it. I know his mind, we spoke of you earlier today, the time is right."

We stopped at the fourth floor, my parent's sanctuary with the nursery in the large front room across the front of the house. We crossed the maple landing through the maid's entrance into the powder room. James stopped to admire the powder room.

"When the house was being finished your grandfather paid a friend of his to steal that marble lion's head from the façade of the mayor's mansion. Finney's mason and plumber then fit the head into the marble there above the middle of that enormous marble tub."

James smiled at my look of surprise and admiration. Gold taps shaped like a lion's paws caused water to pour from the lion's yawning snarl when turned.

"I never walk through here without stopping to chuckle over his daring."

We passed through the powder room, through

mother's dressing room and stopped at a locked closet door. He opened the door with a key from his key ring and turned the crystal knob.

"I've never seen that door opened. Ma's the only one allowed in here. Says she doesn't want her boys mucking up the clean sheets."

James pulled a string and a bare light bulb dimly lit the room. Shelves Stacked with linens surrounded us. He closed and locked the closet door. Crossing to the rear of the large closet, James removed stacks of towels until he exposed the lower third of the rear wall.

Kneeling, James fingered a groove and a catch at the base of a panel like all the others and lifted. With a click, the wall slipped up and latched again into place. Four heavy loaded revolvers hung on brass hooks. A clasp knife and two long bladed Bowie Knives made by James Black dangled next to the gray oily guns. James pocketed the large clasp knife; he began the task of opening the safe.

"In Finney's mind it's impregnable and I agree." Speaking in a low tone, "The wall the safe is actually in is part of the flu for the central chimney. When built, Finney instructed the masons to reinforce the entire height of the chimney with metal bars and extra layers of brick and poured concrete creating a second solid column of masonry to support and enclose the safe. The safe itself was the highest quality available from Philadelphia's Farrell and Company at the time. The mechanical time lock only opens during a specific time of the day. For only for a few minutes. None of the internal mechanism follows a documented pattern."

James looked at me.

"It and the reinforced column were never on the builder's plans. The safe was so large and heavy they brought it into the house on reinforced external scaffolding with a series of block and tackle. The huge size kept it from coming into the house by the front door. It was too big to come up either stairway. It's too heavy for the floors in any room of the house to support, other than the concrete floor of the basement. That's why Finney used a massive scaffold and the block and tackle. They raised it up the height of the house before the walls were finished, leveraged it onto the top of the column, and lowered it into place. The builders enclosed it in the brick and mortar column with iron melted to liquid and poured in place. They created an enclosure that Finney claims can't be broken without tearing a large amount of the top of the house out."

He sat on his bottom in his shirtsleeves.

"We only have twenty minutes, starting one minute ago, to get through the precise numbers and the turns of the dial."

He counted his way around the dial and repeated numbers to himself with silent lips moving. A few minutes left to spare on the mechanical time lock he inserted and turned his key then turned the large brass handle. The door clicked and popped open.

"The external moving parts of the safe's door are brass. By design, they can easily be broken or melted off leaving a safe cracker with a large metal box, dial and handle in their hands or exploded into melted clumps on the floor. Left with a metal box more impregnable than before any attempted cracking."

He sifted through papers and deeds, through official documents pertaining to registered voters and contracts under review by city services. He fingered quickly through compromising letters and photographs of state government officials and industrial magnates. He found the stacks of money they needed.

Handing bricks of paper notes to me, "This next week shall be expensive if we're to start rebuilding Ashbury Heights. We have a lot of people to take care of too."

Pointing to a stack of thick gray rectangles, "These drawers contain jewelry. Most of it belongs to Finney and his widows. Many cameos. He collects women's jewelry in addition to wives and prospect gold."

Finney's mother, father, Finney, and Lucas Pritchard tore most of it from the heart of California in the prospecting days.

The Pritchards trusted the McCurrens to store the manipulative knowledge they collected for business in their safe. Along with their better valuables. With the gold bars were with a few raw nuggets, drawings, and maps of great-grandfather's claim, now a mountain ranch my parents still own. James and my father discussed taking the families to the ranch instead of Sausalito but the trip was too long for little children and neither could be away from the city for long. I stacked the blocks of bank notes on the floor.

Using both hands James closed the door, turned the handle, and removed his key. He checked the watch in his vest pocket and listed to the timer click. He turned the dial until he felt the entire combination reset.

James removed two revolvers from the wall. Lifting his pant leg, he inserted one into his right boot.

"Put this in your pocket where you can get to it quickly," he handed a weapon to me by the barrel.

He took one Bowie Knife out of its sheath and laid it on the floor next to the money. Coat on, James unlatched the wall panel and lowered it into place. He neatly restacked towels in front of the safe and located a small brown satchel, an alligator portmanteau, on a high shelf above. He stacked the banknotes in the bag, placed the fat sharp knife atop the stacks of bills, and locked the bag's large belt through the creaking handles.

An hour after our arrival James Prichard and I left the Buena Vista Avenue house with Edgar Pepper. Rolling down the other side of the hill Edgar pulled over across from the park and pointed at a small animal scuffling around near a clutch of pink-blooming Indian Hawthorn bushes.

He sucked his teeth, "You see that rabbit in the park there Mister Pritchard? Sky so dark it must think it's night and the moon out," suck.

"I'll give five dollars to the man who hits that coney."

Edgar yanked the automobile's parking brake and stood up. He pulled a rifle from under the seat. He sucked his teeth. Quickly aiming he fired at the fat gray rabbit. The shot went wide. The bunny did not notice the men or the bark splintered off the nearby oak.

"Son of a bible lover! Do I get another shot?"

"Only if Thom here misses, you old bastard."

I shouldered the rifle handed to me. Edgar leaned back in his seat covering his ears. After a breath, I fired. The rabbit jumped and scurried away into a thicket.

"Aw ha-ha-ha! Hell you missed too sonny! And with a rifle!"

Edgar laughed, sucked his teeth, and slapped the steering wheel.

"I hit it. I hit its ear. See the blood and fur?"

"Well God damn if he didn't. Why didn't you kill it?" Edgar stopped laughing, sucked his teeth, and glared at me.

"Mister Pritchard said hit it. If he'd said to kill it, I

would have. Hunting from an automobile seems pretty low and lazy to me."

"Well I meant for you to kill it boy," James chuckled.

Pulling an old brown pocketbook from his suit pocket, "okay, here's your five dollars. If you see it again I want you to kill it, understood?"

"If it's hit we could chase it," Edgar sucked his teeth.

"God, if Finney and Lucas were here they would have us out chasing it. They'd chase that rabbit and ring its neck when they caught it. They'd be picking rosemary and little wild onions and garlic all through the chase."

"Finney would make us skin it and dress it. Build him a fire for rabbit stew."

"He'd send someone for water and a cast iron pot and some wild carrots he noticed somewhere. Then he would cut a switch from a strange tree only he recognized and stir his stew with it."

"And Lucas would tell about every rabbit he ever chased and every stew he ever made. He'd roll cigarettes with tobacco he found growing somewhere on a trail or in the woods, dried for a few days in his pocket or on the horn of his saddle. One of those old men would have a half-drunk bottle of whiskey too. Hard whiskey. Trail whiskey they called it, as good for drinking as cleaning wounds. Old men chasing rabbits: Been doing it their whole lives. So have I, either with them or for them."

"Me too," I whispered.

Suck, "rabbit stew sounds tasty," suck. Edgar pointed the rifle at James Pritchard. "Now you two get over near that rabbit's ear and I'll have another go at better aim."

I stared at the skinny deranged-looking little man. James smiled, "Ah ha. Edgar, you lack surprise. I do not. The rifle is empty after those two rabbit shots."

Edgar turned pale, pulled the trigger, barrel poking the lapel of James' smart suit jacket. Nothing happened. James frowned.

"Gimme that money or I'll bash young Thom's head in." He made to turn the rifle around, sucked his teeth and spat tobacco on ivy growing over the curb, smiling to himself.

James pulled the revolver from his boot and, quickly aiming, put a bullet in the stock of Edgar's raised rifle.

Edgar turned white seeing a gun in James Pritchard's hand.

"What's the matter Edgar?" James asked, "You look bad all of a sudden. You surprised to be anticipated?"

Edgar stammered and brown juice dribbled down his chin.

"Thom, take Edgar's rifle." I did, James bullied Edgar out of the automobile and over to pile of house. "We need to act quickly before anyone sees what we're about."

"Don't do it sir," Edgar tried to grab his arm. He looked at me, "He'll kill you too, once he kills me." To James he sucked his teeth, "you son of a bitch, after all I done for you this is what I get?"

"Edgar, someone's been messing with our safe and you're the only man I don't trust who knows where it is."

They walked to the mound where a house stood the day before.

"Wha? Wha? I never touched your safe. I couldn't even ever find the damn thing," Edgar was shaking.

"But you looked and your intention was the same as finding, breaking open, and emptying. If I don't kill you, Thom will. I won't be killing him, you idiot, he's my Godson. His daddy and I are just about brothers. Why do you think I have him with me today? He and his Daddy are the only men I can trust on a day like today."

We worked our feet through house rubble, into a valley of brick and wrenched wood, blocked from sight from the nearby cobbled street and waiting empty automobile. I clutched the alligator satchel and tried to follow the two angry men.

"On a day of disaster normal men can go crazy. Crazy men start thinking of crazy things to do. Friends are shot, wives go missing, husbands find themselves strangled. We saw it in the war. The Spanish War. Once the enemy is conquered, a man in a scene of destruction starts thinking of what he can get away with. Smoke and misery all around, no one will notice after the action. More than one Captain made Major and took command after an officer's body turned up. No one looks at a battlefield and questions who killed whom after the smoke clears. You just collect everyone, regardless of rank.

"Hell Edgar, I smelled your little brain going crazy after the quakes died down and the fires started this morning. I saw in your eyes the barley-veiled mania when I mentioned I needed to get to the house quickly. You never were in a war Edgar. I was. You possessed the same look as a man we knew, and killed, after one of the skirmishes down south.

"We finished defending our position. It was a struggle and we were running low on ammunition when the fighting died down. I gave the order for the men to recover as many rounds as possible from our fallen compatriots and any of the enemy they reached. This was being done when a cry went up from out on the burned hills. An enlisted man, Spokes was his name, Eugene Spokes made himself obvious while taking the possessions off one of our fallen brothers.

"See Edgar, in combat your friend's life and possessions are as sacred as your own. When your brother falls, each man does his best to insure the possessions, along with the man's body, arrive home in tact for his heartbroken loved ones. Spokes looked about in the gloom. In the smoke and the reek of burned flesh, the stench of torn intestines, he decided no one would notice if he started emptying his fallen brother's purse into his own. When they brought him to me, he possessed the look in his eyes I saw in your eyes this morning down in the Avenue Drive, next to the wagon.

"The boys held him and stabbed him to death. We stabbed him with the count of our dead I just read off a piece of scrap paper I clutched in my shaking hand. They cut his throat with the words of the letters I would write for our dead in my head. They cut his throat to make an example of him to the rest of my ravaged, savaged boys. To save a bullet.

"And I wrote a letter that night to his mother. I wrote to her extolling his fine abilities and the heroism we all saw in him in battle the weeks before. I did not write of his lapse in judgment. I wrote he was another on the long list of casualties claimed by the sickness that is war. I won't bore you with the details but you are much easier to kill. I don't have to write anything after you are dead. Letters of the dead are a daunting task, the largest tangible drawback of command.

"Now march your sorry self on over to that demolished water closet so I can shoot you. Oh, and give Thom your badge, Edgar. You are no longer a deputy."

Mumbling under his breath Edgar fished in his pockets and tossed me a dulled pewter badge. Edgar stood in a white pile of rubble tile near a long cast iron tub. He sucked his teeth and glared as James Pritchard lifted his gun and shot him squarely in the chest.

"Thomas McCurren, hold that badge and raise your right hand and repeat after me: I Thomas McCurren, do solemnly swear that I will faithfully execute all lawful precepts directed to a marshal of the district of Northern California under the authority of the United States and true returns make; and in all things well and truly and without malice or partiality perform the duties of the office of marshal's deputy of the district of Northern California during my continuance in said office and take only my lawful fees. So help me God."

I repeated what my father's best friend, my Godfather, told me to say. I was unclear what was happening. My mind was still thinking of men dead in battle long ago and far away.

We stumbled back over the splintered house. "We'll run you for sheriff once the city shakes off some of her dust and gets rebuilt a little."

In the automobile, James behind the steering wheel, "It's going to be a glorious time my boy. Nothing like a disaster to galvanize the people. We'll each help the other get past the tragedy and rebuild our neighborhood, and each other. In a time of crisis each person must attempt to remain level headed; a person can make the worst decisions or no decisions, as long as they keep a level head they will come through every problem a-okay."

He released the parking brake and we coasted down the hill.

"Edgar back there never was one for a level head. Or thinking very much. If he admitted what he was planning to do today and whom he was planning to do it with, he would still be driving this fine automobile. Once a man like that goes against you completely, there is no return. He'll just wait until a time of weakness presents itself and stab you in the throat. Let's take a turn down to the Avenue Drive, load up with supplies, then head downtown and see if we cannot locate your father. Let him know you all are a-okay. I suppose you could tell him about the Spencers. Better he hear it from you than anyone else. You can tell him about Edgar Pepper and the safe too. Nothing you have seen today is a secret from your family or will surprise them, understand?"

Chapter Five

After stocking the backseat with bandages, rations, dark bottles of cold coffee and leather buckets of water, we bumped our way across paving stones loosed and rearranged by the quakes. We traversed the damage and eventually drove down a deserted Market Street. I kept the reloaded rifle where anyone we passed could see.

We lurched over small fissures and hills in the street until sentries stopped us at the fire line. The roar of the blaze was close enough now we needed to speak loud and clear. Each man tied at least one handkerchief around his face to keep the acrid smoke from throat and lungs. Eyes streamed, filth covered us. The sky was black. I reckon we drove straight into hell after sundown.

"We're in as far as they allow automobiles," James told me close to my ear, yelling over the distant roar of the fire and the orders of the firefighters. "Any closer and the engine will blow up or the tires will burst. You take as much food and water as you can carry. I'll take as many injured men out as I can. Go find your father and I'll help the medical folks load the automobile."

We shook hands and James tied the packs of food around my shoulders. I carried more blankets under my arms and clutched a heavy wine bottle of coffee in either hand.

"You see any of those Edison newsreel gentlemen or photographers; send them back here to me on the double."

"Yes sir!" I hollered as I shuffled away down a blackened street covered in rubble. I asked anyone I saw where Lieutenant McCurren's crew was. They pointed me into the heart of the blaze. "The L.T. is down at Van Ness. You're close. Follow these hoses and you'll find him and his men."

"Send any injured men you have back now," I told each person I found. "We have an automobile to carry the worst; they'll be sending more men with automobiles and wagons from Saint Mary's."

I rushed low through the stinging smoke wishing I could crawl to keep track of the route of the hoses. The west wind picked up. It stirred the soot, ash, and heavy smoke but cleared nothing. The water and steam thickened the air as I approached what I hoped was Van Ness Street. Landmarks, familiar since childhood, were either gone or unrecognizable. I stumbled over bodies. Men, women, and children: still and lifeless. Crushed then recovered, abandoned, some partially burned. "Why don't they stink?" They did, the strong smell of filth mingled with the stench of burned death.

"No wonder the priests go on about hell-fire as the wage for sin," I thought, "this truly is miserable. No other human experience could ever be as horrific as this. At least the quakes stopped. I imagine this will never cease."

I crouched, passing along a line of dead and dying feet. I thought James Pritchard's tale of pilfered war dead and wondered if these men would merit respect or be picked clean by the sinister carrion who must surely accompany every living hell. In answer to my thoughts, I spied a priest and a medic working leapfrog down the row of moaning bodies. The medic with a large glass syringe he filled from a clear bottle. The priest with vestments and last rights he soaked in a bottle I assume filled with Holy Water. Each took his turn depending on which side of death the next victim laid closest.

I hailed the medic and the priest and asked them where the Lieutenant was. Both pointed into the source of the gloom. There was a deafening boom and a shower of rubble pelted us. We fell across the injured and covered our own heads with our hands as bricks fell all around. A thudding sound was interspersed with the wet scrunching sound of bodies absorbing crushing blows. Debris staved-in the head of the medic. His brains and blood covered the chest of a panting young boy who laid next in the row, feet pointing in unnatural opposite directions.

The priest jumped to the medic and, after saying his last rights, handed the large glass syringe and unbroken bottle to me.

"Give two thick lines worth to each anywhere you can get the needle in, not in the chest. Not in a limb that will need to be removed. Do not poke yourself and try to avoid getting any on your skin. Now!"

I stared, uncomprehending, at the priest for a moment. Smears of red streaked his pale face where he quickly wiped away the blood of other men and sweaty grime.

"I'm looking for my father," I stammered.

The exhausted, demented looking priest, painted in the blood of others scared me.

"These people are all looking for their Father you damn jackass!" He hollered, "Now take that syringe in hand to the next man or I will strangle the life out of you with these holy ribbons while I whisper your last rights and choke the breath from your body!" I knew he meant to. I saw it would not be the first time that day the priest strangled someone with the holy cloth.

"Yes Father."

I removed my packs and took the syringe from the priest. I filled it from the bottle and moved to the boy. The priest crawled past us to the man after with a stern look of recognition, the man's body held a clump of white cracked subway tiles and mortar, half resting, half protruding from his chest. The tiles, like the priest's face, were dotted and streaked with the dark rivulets of the blood of the dead. The man was alive.

The priest took the man's hand in his, in a stern voice he spoke, "Lanny Furrow. You were an evil and corrupt man in life. This is the hell you shall remain in the center of for eternity. The abuse you laid on you poor family. The beating of that sweet child to death. The ruin of your wife's family business so you could gamble and run with the whores and degenerates has brought you here. The filth you spoke to me the last time you were in our church: I can still hear your nasty words gnawing in my ears. It has all caught up to you.

"I am here to help usher you into an eternity of misery and torturous fire. Engulfing licks of flame will meticulously peal the charring flesh from your bones with excruciating pain repeatedly, again and again and again. You will feel the burning refreshed every minute in a forever of minutes. It is entirely your own fault. You will not receive mercy you Godless wretch. Justice is your reward. Your eternal reward. The soul of that poor boy you killed in your drunken rage will be pissed down your worthless throat and intoxicated by its sting you will forever be repenting in vain in a world of coals and ash and fire."

The priest looked me in the eye.

"We do not waste our precious morphine on this worthless son of a bitch, my boy. Do you have a knife or a gun or any weapon in your pockets?"

"No father," not trusting the priest I lied.

"Pity, would have been easier."

To the injured wretch, "Now Lanny, I won't be giving

the last rights to you. It would be a waste of my breath and God's ears to attempt to preserve you from the glorious flaming justice your rotten and pathetic soul so rightly and richly deserves."

He said this as he looked through the broken man's pockets for any kind of weapon. Finding a clasp knife, he sat back on his heels. He opened the blade and scraped the meat of his thumb across its sharp edge. He handed the knife to me.

"This is a very fine knife. French. A fire brigade knife, if I am not mistaken. No doubt, stolen or won through God knows what kind of immoral and lascivious pursuit. Now my boy, we waste no more time on a cur all too well known to me for his illegal and evil deeds. Cut his throat and we will see to the rest of these poor souls. You may keep the knife since you claim you have none of your own," he still offered the open knife to me. My mind reeled.

"Father, help me please. I came down here to find my father and now I am to act as your assassin. Could you please let me be on my way to find my father? Perhaps you could strangle him as you offered to strangle me?"

The priest looked at me and smiled. Through the gloom, he studied my face. He looked down at the black oily water washing past us from the fire hoses. It washed the blood into the gutters and drained away at the sides of the street. I watched his gaze and thought of the blood and soot flowing into the bay absorbed and diluted by the mass of the Ocean.

"My boy, none of us is where we expected to be this day. I did not plan to find so many of my fine friends and congregation dead today. I did not expect to be helping God by taking the evil He laid in front of me, from this world. I will not waste an opportunity put forth by God to clean the world of one evil man who, while alive, spread rot to all unfortunate enough to come into contact with."

White spittle formed at a corner of the holy man's mouth.

"I have known this man since he was a boy. I watched as he slowly killed his parents by repeatedly breaking their hearts. I witnessed his corrupting influence on girl after girl. I stood by and was unable to act as he began grinding his own children under the heel of his soulless boot. He killed his own son. A flaxen-headed little trooper. In a drunken passion not more than a month ago. I stood, useless, over the grave of the savaged three-year-old innocent."

Tears stood in his tired eyes.

"Before they lowered the coffin into the cool earth I opened the lid. I made them stop the process of burial. I fell to my knees and opened the little lid of the little coffin and I saw. I saw the hole in the poor babe's head where this man threw him against the cook stove. I saw the work the poor undertaker embarked upon but failed at by no fault of his own. God knows the flesh is weak in life but it is literally so much weaker in death. I closed the lid after my tears fell upon the cheeks of the poor lamb. I walked away.

"In my rage I left his weak mother and five other bruised, miserable children. My impotence engulfed me. Her impotence enraged me. I asked God to do what He thought best. I gave myself to my God and I now have the chance to finish His work. This is my life. There are no surprises. I do not care who must die today.

"The innocent and worthy suffer every day. It is the evil whose experiences are an exception in any of God's natural disasters. Perhaps God creates disaster to clean the earth. Innocents have perished today. Innocents perish every day. If a few of the worst perish too then perhaps the death of the good is not in vain.

"Can you not see? This is an opportunity for justice in a Biblical manner. You have the opportunity to participate in a cleansing of the earth. This man needs to die a violent death. He needs to die horribly, miserably, alone. Without a Samaritan, without a champion, without a wailing woman pleading for His mercy. He needs to die at the hands of a stranger!"

"Father," my mind tumbled with thought, "if you or I cut his throat someone may discover his mangled body." I reasoned quickly with the crazed priest, "if it appears he was murdered it might come back on either one of us. What if he died in a way keeping with circumstances? Perhaps this mass of tile and grout and mortar?"

The priest's eyes lit, "a fine idea my boy. You keep the knife. It's not engraved with anything telling, is it?"

I took the proffered blade, studied it closely.

"Put it in your pocket and help me bash his brains with this clump of rock."

I stood with the priest and together we wrenched the jagged and bloody boulder from the man's chest. When we held it between us and were astride Lanny Furrow the priest whispered what sounded to Thom like a quick prayer and said, "Now."

We dropped the mass of bloody tiles onto the man's sweaty, wide-eyed writhing head. His face disappeared in a wet and fatal squelch. Blood covered our boots.

"Pax Deo," the priest said. "I will be pleased to tell his family, when next I see them, of my regrettable discovery of his poor pathetic body recognizable only by the stains of

Satan on his lazy and worthless limbs."

I noticed the tattoos on the crushed man's arms. They were not drawings that appealed to a man given to a kind disposition and selfless action. The priest began searching under his mantle until he came up with a large bottle of whiskey.

"Sit here. Leave the mess of Lanny Furrow. Have a tired dram with an old man."

We sat in the haze and traded the bottle of burning liquor until I felt the lazy warmth permeate the stink and filth that now penetrated deep into my bones.

"Quickly offer me your confession so this may be behind you." I did as instructed and the priest listened, and then spoke. My forgiveness was rapid.

"Father Augustine," the priest smiled, offered his hand, "you must be Lieutenant McCurren's oldest, Thomas."

I took the proffered hand.

"I am Thomas McCurren, father."

Father Augustine kept a tight, knuckled grasp on my hand and leaned close.

"You have been a brave lad today," he whispered. "God shall not forget you. I shall not forget you. If you tell anyone what we did to that man, I will find you and strangle the breath from your body. You understand me, correct?"

I smelled the man's rank sour breath and felt his whiskers against my ear.

"I promise, I will never tell anyone of the things I have done today. I am sure no one would believe me if I did."

Hand released he took another choking sip from the bottle.

"I never imagined I would be threatened by a priest. Twice."

Father Augustine laughed.

"A passive clergy is a sin against God and humanity. The day the clergy relegate themselves to listening and watching, not acting, is the day the people invent their heroes and turn their backs on God and church. If we do not act for God in the affairs of women and men, who will? The police? The politicians? The military? No, it is the clergy who possess the knowledge of the human spirit and the knowledge of sin. The day the clergy devolve into passive, hand wringing problem-watchers is the day the clergy themselves turn on their parishioners and become yet another myriad problem within a crumbling, rotten society. Clergy who counsel and do not act, they are perpetuators, perpetrators of sloth and envy.

"You were surprised by what we did? I promise I am no exception. More the rule. We call it Judicious Theology. We are not the passive watchers of problems you imagine. Nor are we the hand-wringing old ladies whispering to the law about problems seen and suspected. We do indeed perpetuate that image. Aesthetics, while not a waste of time, are still a consumption of time. All images are false. That is why we call them images; they are imagined.

"Many a just act is perpetrated at the hands of my brothers and sisters. Next time you learn of the death of someone, someone you knew was a corrupt bastard, ask if his priest was at hand at the passing. We read many a seemingly recovered sickbed inevitable last rites despite the best encouraging efforts put forth by family and physician. I wish helping the good remain on this earth was so easily accomplished as removing the evil.

"Do the nuns know about "Judicious Theology" being practiced by their priests?"

Father Augustine laughed again.

"Of course they do my boy. What an innocent you are. Our hospitals serve the good of all. We save lives and help the women have their babies, we treat all kinds of illness. We also clear evil from the earth. My God. Of course the sisters know. They are much less scrupulous than we poor priests when it comes to issues of justice."

"But how do you know what you're doing is right?"

"I'll give you an honest answer: No one knows what is right or wrong in this world. All decisions, all perceptions are subjective. However, the first clue, in life, to know if you are doing right, is opportunity. An amiable thief I once took confession from told me of the theft of an expensive tea service from one of the downtown hotels. He said, "I was walking down the alley on my way to get tight at the Pub. I looked over and the back door of the hotel's restaurant was standing wide. I peaked in and a gleaming silver service was sitting on a back counter. Ready for the cupboard. No one was about. The gas light at the end of the alley sputtered and extinguished as I stood there looking about. So I nicked it. Would have got away with it if my cousin hadn't been greedy on the fence and turned me in over his share of the take."

"His point is my point: If circumstance leads you to opportunity, treat the situation as the first indication you are on the correct path. If twenty people tell me, in confidence, the evil ways of a man, if I see his destructive ways over the course of his life, if providence sends him to one of our hospital beds with a legitimate illness, I promise you, I communicate his history and habits to the laudable sisters if they are not already aware.

"If he is offered to us without manipulated circumstances and we find the chance without any footling around, the man may end up with the wrong medicine. He may drown in his bath. He may have an aneurism. Air bubbles in the blood stream by hypodermic are quickly administered, frantically fatal. All very tragic. All very easy to portray as tragedy. Perhaps the good and the innocent will be preyed upon a little less. Remember, we of the church possess no Hippocratic Oath. We are bound only to serve God."

The father stood slowly and stretched his short legs.

"Go find your father my boy. I will take the syringe and morphine with my vestments, preserving the living, attending the dead and dying, on my own." On our feet, Father Augustine locked my hand in his warm and rigid grasp. "Remember, I am Father Augustine. I suspect you and a few others may qualify as Saints before the end of this, the longest of days our city has ever seen."

Taking a final deep draught of the whiskey, Father Augustine handed me the bottle.

"The men you meet further in will need this more than I. I want you to know, I want to tell you: Finney McCurren, Laurence McCurren, and James Pritchard are three of the finest men I have ever known. I respect them each and hope you do too. When you find your father, give him that bottle, and tell him August needs more morphine."

I mumbled a self-conscious thank you as the priest shambled away to his line of injured and dying. I buttoned the bottle into my shirt and tightened my belt to keep it from slipping out. I regained my packs of food, blankets, and bottles of coffee.

Hunching and thinking about the long thin French knife in my jacket pocket, I followed the path the hoses snaked along the waves of disturbed paving stones. The sounds of men, noise, and the blaze grew louder as I approached a clearing in the center of Market Street.

Here, as on many other streets, the paving stones between the streetcar tracks remained flat, intact. Standing between rails in the Van Ness intersection I spied my father shouting through a dented megaphone. His face was black, his hands wrapped in once-white cloth bandage

Chapter Six

My Da, Lieutenant Laurence McCurren, was a strong and powerful man raised in the pride of the San Francisco fire department. He too was in the war. He died more than once in the fires of the city. His men respected him, his superiors watched him. All envied his luck. His family and community adored him. He was quick with unbelievable crazy stories of his father's days living in the wilds of California digging and panning with "The Fever."

Gold attracted my great grandfather, Finney McCurren, to The Western Edge of the New World. Love of the land and one of the woman raised on that land kept him there. Long before dirt and rocks inevitably replaced the treasure, love replaced "The Fever" with a stronger amorous fever.

Laurence was quick with praise for his men and us his children. He was a drinker who became jovial and more intelligently talkative the more he drank. He was generous, friendly, and proud.

"This city offers no finer occupation to boy or man than saving her and her people from the devastation of fire, lads. It is a dangerous job." My father says, recounting his days in the scrub starving, panning with the fever, rifle at the ready to run off natives, Spaniards, Americans and bandits, "Where is the fun in life without a bit of danger, eh? Not dangerous enough for me, otherwise I never would have married Angela!"

Laurence, always kidding, always teasing so long as no feelings got hurt. He stood as large and as strong as the shifted stone pillars now splintered all over the city, up and down the state, once stood.

At the edge of the enormous fire time receded. The

sky, blacker than night looked alive with bits of burning debris. When an ember landed on your clothes and burned through it felt like a sting from a very large, haunted wasp.

This did not happen to the firefighters who wore their protective gear. Instead their boots fill with boiling water, soaking, softening and ballooning their feet. Arms become numb with the work of hoisting and heaving the heavy hoses and pumping water into flames. The roar of the blaze absorbed all sound and speech. On some of the men had dried blood caked about their ears and necks. Eardrums burst in the blasts of dynamite used in an attempt to create a burn perimeter and contain the fire.

Everywhere the stinking and charred remains of quake and fire victims oozed. No priest attended the lumps of feted humanity. Exhausted men, blackened and coughing soot stepped over or around the dead as more displaced paving stones.

The brigade grew hungry, thirsty, and exhausted with nowhere to go to the toilet, nowhere safe to grab a few minutes rest when relieved by others. All eyes were red rimmed and swollen. Noses bled with irritation from the smoke. All hacked and coughed a miracle within each labored breath.

Laurence McCurren spied me resting on my haunches talking with some of his lads. He saw the packs of food and the bottles of coffee. He called to his second and left him in charge. A bottle was going around, a few sputtered with the burn of the brown drink on their raw and blistered throats.

"Everyone okay Thomas?" Laurence asked with the anxiety of a separated parent briefly reunited with his real life.

"We're all fine. The house has a bit of damage but its minor compared to others in the neighborhood."

"Good, good."

To a briefly choking man made my father say, "Now don't you be spitting fine liquor out like that Gregory Martin. We'll have no alcohol abuse in my company, not in the line of duty, no matter the burn or the blood in your throat."

They all smiled. The bottle went to the Lieutenant and he threw his head back, warm brown sting gurgled down his raw throat. With the back of his hand, he wiped dribble off his chin and around his face.

"I take it you found the priest and the medic, Thomas? Our little priest is partial to this brand. His good brothers in the East freight it to him by the case."

"Yes sir," I looked up at my father, "your medic is dead. Debris from an explosion bashed his head in. The priest seemed the sort who could handle both roles by himself. He sent me along to find you and your men. Back at the perimeter James Pritchard had an automobile and was moving some of the worse off to the church and the Avenue Drive."

"Did it look like a teamster could make it in here? With the right horses?"

"Yes sir."

"Well then, when you get back you find anyone in charge and tell them to send up a long wagon with food and some medical aid. If they can get two or three horses and a wagon of reinforcements up here over the mounds and through the debris we can butcher one of the horses and cook it right here. No lack of fuel or fire. The other horses can take our exhausted and light casualties back out."

"Mister Pritchard is coming back for me, I'll let him know. We'll organize it for you."

"Good lad. You and James see to it then."

He stood, stretched, we walked together.

"Ma and the rest are in Sausalito by now. At Abigail Pritchard's brother's estate. It's where we're headed too, before nightfall."

Silently we studied the rubble and oil-slicked water flowing and flowering over the pavement.

"Da, they want me to tell you. The Spencers are gone. I found the baby. He was dead. James's men located Mister and Missus Spencer later. They died in the biggest of the quakes this morning. I found Baby, still in his crib. Warm and nestled up as if he were a peaceful, sleeping little thing. Ma was just about crazy with the sadness. We all were."

Father looked at me as though I was speaking another language and I thought, for a moment, I was. The language of death was one I only overheard on the mouths of adults. Children and the boys I knew did not talk of death seriously, only as a plaything. Adults spoke of death. They spoke of it shyly. Low and quiet amongst themselves.

The lieutenant was stunned. So much death. So many good men down. Neighbors and lifelong acquaintances never seen again. In the war, death was so thick. It was another facet of life. Like eating or urinating. Death was an abstraction as a civilian, as a firefighter. An occasional event never considered. Never anticipated or expected save isolated, tragic circumstances.

Now it was back. Again, death and fear surrounded him more than love. Suddenly the peace he and his fellow patriots fought so hard to preserve and sustain was gone.

It never occurred to him to fear for friends or their families. He feared for his own family. Of course, they were safe, he told himself all day. An unrealistic thought but the only one worth entertaining on a morning of unrelenting terror and disaster. The only thought able to sustain him at his post. With his men. To keep him from scurrying through debris filled streets over hills of devastation to his Dear Ones.

The birth of little Abigail flooded his mind. The months of the swollen belly. His little wife who looked like an Amazon snake after swallowing a boar glimpsed in a flickering newsreel.

Her grumpiness in their bedroom, "I am too hot. Get away from me. You are making me hot!"

Shoving him almost entirely out of their bed onto the cold floor with suddenly powerful scrawny arms and legs. Followed a few minutes later by, "Oh Laurence. I am so cold. Get over here and warm me up!"

Her warm swollen body. Always primed for their love.

Her obsession with smell. Only a pregnant nose possibly smelled what she smelled.

"What is that smell? What have you been eating? Get away from me with that vial smell!"

She ordered children about the house opening windows and doors to exhaust an odor only she and the baby who squirmed deep inside her could possibly smell.

It was the same for Donald and Louisa. They courted pregnancy for so many years. They were such a happy pair, even happier with their little baby. Laurence was the boy's Godfather. They were in the McCurren's and the Pritchard's houses as often as they were at home.

Donald was a friend since before Laurence recalled. They met, Louisa and Donald, during Angela's and his wedding. Louisa grew up with Angela and Abigail on Nob Hill. Now the little family was gone.

Laurence pictured his new little baby girl he held in

one hand only a few month ago. Moist, red, and dark with fine hair and long parchment fingernails. The peaceful sleep of an exhausted mother. Spent father. Well fed newborn. Together on clean sheets. Thomas and the boys out in the park playing ball, attending the cinema, or playing at a neighbor's house. Their return home, to the quiet house of a new baby escorted by Pritchards. With the makings for sandwiches and hot potatoes, growlers of beer, fine cigars.

The center of all the Spencer's time and all their energy now gone. The pity of loss in the survivor's life. A familiar emptiness filled only by memories. The expectation of sweet little children growing into fine adults now abruptly false. Tears ran down his face.

"You're a good boy Thomas. There is nothing you could do. We are all okay?"

"Yes sir. Ma and the three are with the Pritchards in Sausalito."

"Where are Finney and Margie? Any word of the giddy newlyweds?"

"I have no idea where they are. Finney sent a telegram last night before their train left Los Angeles. I figure they were somewhere in the middle of the state or across the bay when the worst of it hit. Maybe they got as far Oak-Land. There's no contacting the line and folks say the damage is all over the state."

"Do they? I suppose they're better off than anyone else we know. Probably making the barman in the club car crazy with their early morning drunk bickering."

I smiled.

"Well then, she's waiting for you. Go to your Ma. Give her my love. We expect to be relieved shortly. I'll run back to the Buena Vista house for a snooze and a meal and be back down here again late this evening. You come find me later today at the house. I know there's more to talk about; I see it in your face. You have to go now; I have to get back to work. Trust James Pritchard, you know he's my brother."

We were among the spent brigade boys and sergeants, now feeling the effects of their exhaustion and the mellowing whiskey.

"Leave this bottle for us, eh boy? And send more down on that wagon."

Chapter Seven

Finney "First Punch" McCurren was indeed making the barman in the club car crazy. Finney and Margie were in the club car all night and returned before the sun rose hot over the dusty plains of Central California. Green glowing mountains towered far off in the west as the train sped north through dusty towns with no names. People with no English or Spanish looked up from their tasks as the train passed. They worked the dark earth everyday of their lives. One day the dark earth would bury them. California caked their hair and was under their nails. California was in their clothes and firm beneath thin woven blankets they slept on every night.

They watched the trains pass and never wondered where they came from or where they went. Finney and Margie sat on the train, watched the sturdy dirty faces pass in the fields, and never wondered where they came from or where they were going.

"Where the hell is that fellow? I told him we'd be here first thing and by God, it is first thing. I want a cup. I know you could use one too."

Finney McCurren was an impatient man where coffee was concerned. Skinny and sun burned tough, he wore expensive tailored suits cut in a Western style and cowboy boots made from exotic animal skins. Today he wore yellow Ostrich. His large hat sat on the bar. He rubbed his hard chin with a rough a callused hand and scratched himself with horny old yellow fingernails.

"Where is that poor deputy U.S. Marshal sitting, Finney?" Margie asked.

She was a beautiful red haired woman who turned heads. Her skin was pale and lips were dark. Her green eyes made Finney go weak in the knees. He was much older than she was but neither of them seemed aware of it.

"I'll make the coffee and take him a cup too."

"Well I was going to do that," Finney said, "but there ain't no coffee grinder back there."

"I can grind the beans, hand me a skillet and I'll roast them until they pop."

Finney walked around the bar and handed her a small iron skillet.

"Deputy Doolen and that bastard he has in custody are in the last car afore the Caboose. Has the man manacled to a pipe on the wall. Damn waste of time. If I were still a deputy I'd shoot that snake in the head while we passed over one of those gulches and toss him off the back of the train. Then I'd find me some nice widder woman to pass the rest of the train ride with in comfort."

"I know that is exactly the thing you did and would still do. I know that is why you have not been a peace officer for over fifty years. You lost sight of the peace and only cared about the officer part by the time they retired you."

The coffee beans were growing hot.

"No one retired me woman. I quit. Hell, things were easier before statehood. Much easier before those damn fools joined us up to the rest of the nation. You're too young to recall but Goddamn if we didn't have a hell of a time before they went and mucked it all up. Hell, only reason the Federal boys from the United States of America wanted California was to tax the gold we found out at Sutter's. Sutter's changed everything. Some for the good. Some for the bad. California was big enough to be her own country, maybe two or three countries. She still is.

"Why are coffee beans called beans? They are not beans. They are berries. Why are they not called coffee berries?"

"And the ports. Can't forget they wanted our ports. I have no idea. I'll start calling them coffee berries now though. First time I ever drank coffee they called them beans. It was with the old Governor, long time ago. Did I ever tell you the time I almost shot the Governor? That was before he was Governor. He was a piss-ant lawyer for a dirty son of a bitch we grabbed up for rape. Governor Bigler told me shoot the fellow's client right out in front of the state capital building. We just come down from the mountains a few months before. Lucas and I were on our way to San Francisco but met up with some of those fine Spanish women who kind of lived around Benicia in those days."

"Whores."

As the coffee berries sizzled and popped Margie crushed them vigorously with the back of a large silver spoon.

"Well now God damn it, there's no reason to start calling women names. Especially ladies you never met and are probably dead and buried. If she was like that, I never knew it. I never gave her no money. I did buy here a fine horse and wagon. A bunch of dresses. I paid for her room at an Inn there in town for a few months, but I was a staying there in it with her. Oh, and I guess I did get a little drunk and shoot some fellow tried to move in on her and me. Hell, I'd forgot all about that fellow. Tall he was. Shot him right in the neck for her. She did like the mattress polka I have to admit. She was good at the mattress polka."

"Mattress tango."

"God damn."

"If she was Spanish I doubt she knew how to polka. If she was Spanish she probably did a mean mattress tango."

"I need a woman with a mean mattress waltz."

"You have her, and more."

Finney smiled, "We were a bit rough in those days. Living in the mountains with my Pa after Ma died hadn't taught us much about the finer points of men and women. Lucas Pritchard and I only came down out of them hills after the bandits killed my Pa. We never did find the bunch what killed him. That was why I took the law job in Benicia with Lucas. All the gold we dug out and cashed in taught us the nature of Man though, all right.

"We came out of those mountains with enough to buy that little town from the Spaniards. I never lost one ounce to treachery. My Pa taught us how to conceal what we owned; the lesson took after watching him get it in the chest in the dust on the scrubby side of that damn hill.

"Only piece of metal aside from that gold I still can put my hands on from when I was a growing up is that damn deputy U.S. Marshal's badge. It's in my steamer in our car. It's heavy too. Like to rip a hole in every shirt I wore it on. That's why we all wore leather vests. Badges don't rip leather as easy. Vest keeps a man warm when it's cool and cool when it's warm.

"Lucas and I were two of the first law men in Benicia. Only been a town for a few years, there was always military all over the place. They wanted to move the state capital from San Jose to Benicia and it wouldn't do to have fellows killed and robbed in the hotels. Or out in the road from Sacramento.

Margie finished crushing the coffee berries and scooped them into the boiling skillet. Finney stared out the window at the landscape passing in the dark.

"Too much gold dust swirling around in everyone's brains to have any good sense left. Once we arrested a woman who killed a dirt farmer for what amounted to the price of a drink at the bar.

"Worse were the boys who'd been out prospecting with no luck for so long they forgot the laws of men. Or forgot not to ignore them. Any fellow who came out those mountains, whether he got his claim or the claim got him, if he headed to San Francisco he was fair game for the lawless.

"Once we come across a man who was torn to pieces. Literally, pieces. We found the fellow who did it to him just down the trail apiece, sleeping under an oak. Blood all over him. The dead man's stink still on him. We woke the man and asked him about the dead fellow. I remember he never blinked. I learned right there, anytime you come cross a fellow who doesn't blink you need to watch him. Whole time we were talking to him from up on our horses he never once blinked his eyeballs. Sounds like a small thing but it was eerie. I recall it now as one of the oddest things from those days.

"Didn't help that he insisted there was gold dust in the other man's belly. Claimed he just couldn't cut in deep enough with his knife to find it. Therefore, he used his hands. Said if we showed him where the body was he'd share the take with us when he finally dug it out the man's carcass. I shot him right there. Lucas Pritchard and I buried those two poor sons of bitches out there by the side the road. Buried them together so the torn up fellow could maybe mess with the crazy one's soul for the rest of eternity.

"So there Lucas Pritchard and I were in front the fine new state capitol building holding Latham Neeley, man we all knew raped three young women by the name of Pope. He snuck onto the Pope's land one Wednesday night when he knew the parents were off at church. The Popes left their three girls at home alone because the youngest, Mary Pope, who was seventeen, was ill with a head cold. The other two girls stayed at the house to look after their kid sister.

"Well, the Popes head out to church and no sooner do they leave but the two girls who weren't sick hear a knock at the front door. Thinking it was a neighbor they open the door to find this nasty bastard standing there drunk, stinking, and smoking a cigar fellows used to roll themselves. They fell apart into burning bits all over the ground while you were a smoking it.

"Twist cigar we called it. You might be riding along and see a bit of stray tobac plant with its larger leaves dropped over and dried out. You jump off your horse and mosey over, cut those leaves off. Roll them up, twist the ends to light, and suck. Needed to use a string to hold it together otherwise, it all fell apart, spittle wouldn't hold for long.

"Anyway, afore either girl, and these were girls you see, young ones about nineteen and twenty. Before either sister could think or even spit, that son of a bitch punched the one in the face and tossed the other down hitting her head so hard on their stone floor she never did regain herself. He dragged the one he punched, the twenty year old, and tossed her onto the Pope's supper table. Raped her right there on the dishes and cloth the girls were fixing to clear when the knock came at the door.

Margie interrupted, "Let's just say he raped the girls. I do not want to hear the misogynistic intricacies detailing the crime of some jackass you ended up killing. It is bad enough he bothered them and you were later involved. I do not want to know all you know. I'm still thinking of the man who did not blink."

Finney looked genuinely surprised.

"I am sorry Margie. I saw so much I kind of forgot

what civilians do and do not want to know. Only fellow I ever really talked about any of this with was Lucas and he was there with me so we never glossed over any details. I promise, I get in too much detail you just let me know and I'll put a cork in it."

She smiled, "I doubt that."

"Let me see. He raped and killed the two older girls. He was a piece of work. After finding some brandy Mister Pope kept, he got more drunk. Those girls each looked as pretty as their Mama did. Shiny hair and fine skin. The Popes were fine folks from Pennsylvania. Mister Pope was a supply fellow with the Army. A civilian who only did trade with the military.

"Drunker still he starts to looking for the valuables he assumed every Californian kept in their house no matter how modest the house. The Popes were hard working folks but like most that never prospected or took advantage of their neighbor, Mister Pope never owned a spare plug nickel to piss on. Hell, kid's use up all a fellow's money faster than a lawfully wedded woman. Even if he can get any extra money together. I've heard tell daughters use it up worse than sons do when it comes to needing to buy things.

Margie made a fist and said, "Have you ever heard about getting punched in the nose by a woman while drinking her coffee on a train in the middle of the night?"

"Okay, okay. So this son of a bitch is going through the house tearing everything apart thinking he's gonna find a stash of gold and jewels. Instead, he finds a sleeping Jenny Pope. She slept through the entire time he's been in their house. He makes sure she don't sleep any longer. When the Ma and Pa come home, they find their daughters dead in the front rooms and their house a holy wreck. Missus Pope ran to the back of the house to their youngest daughter's room where she found the man. Apparently, he strangled the poor girl while he was raping her.

"The Ma told us later the air left her body. She was so upset but then there he was. There was Mister Pope walking in with his long rifle, tears rolling down his stricken face, aiming to kill the man and firing into the man's chest from no more than a foot away.

"Hammer fell but misfired. Latham Neeley, they told me later, grinned with ash dropping down his shirtfront. A halo of smoke trickled out from the corner of his spittle-wet lips. He stood up, red and pink shiny prick still hard and now pointed at them. He pulled up and fastened his britches. He spit on their floor and walked right past the Popes without a word. Broke Mister Pope's jaw with a punch from his elbow and Missus Pope's left arm with a wrench from his fist as Mister Pope and then Missus Pope tried to stop him from leaving.

"Now everyone in Benicia knew the Popes and the Neeleys. They were all good folks except that son of bitch oldest son of the Neeley's, Latham. When we found out, Lucas Pritchard and I went and got Latham at the saloon on the main road out from town. He knew why we were there. I started to draw my gun. I was gonna crack him on his noggin so Lucas could buy me a drink.

"Who was there drinking with him and insisting to come along to the jail, just to make sure nothing violent happened to his client on the way? His lawyer. Ever notice how "lawyer" and "liar" sound just alike if you spit them out of your mouth as if you have bad taste or a wiry hair stuck in your throat? If you say them the way you might if a little bug flew in your mouth and you spit it out? Lawyer. It's a growly sounding kind of word.

"My daddy was a lawyer," Margie said smiling.

"I forgot that: Finest class of people I ever met; liars."

She smiled and Finney continued.

"Now, I possessed no qualms over killing a rapist and his lawyer in them days, same thing as killing a rapist on his lonesome. Not Lucas Pritchard. He kept on at me about how Mister Johnson done nothing wrong. How Mister Johnson was really a nice fellow. I knew the real reason though; Lucas always kept a tighter grip on money than a wooden Indian did a handful of wooden cigars.

"He didn't want to pay any part of the burial fee for either of them. I told Lucas lawyering for a man like Neeley made the one doing the lawyering just as guilty as the rapist. I also told him I thought it was wrong to be drinking with a man, lawyer, or no lawyer, who just done what Neeley did to the poor Pope girls. If you're going to hang with the wrong fellows in this life, you might as well expect to be hanged with them to death.

"Young Lucas was high minded and I let him talk me out of shooting the pair of them in the bar. Or on the way back to town. The blood of the girls was still on Latham, on his hands and on his shirt. That was burning at me.

We got back to town just as the Judge, our boss, and Governor Bigler, his boss, were walking to take their lunch at Miss Nick's.

Miss Nick ran a nice lunch place. Used to be down on the water there in old Benicia. Old Widder Nick birthed so many children that when they all growed up she kept the tables and cook pots and continued on cooking the same amount of food, she just started charging money to folks from town. They saw us approaching, stopped, and waited.

We told them what happened. Told them where we found Latham and introduced them to his lawyer. They both knew him.

Judge looked at me, asking with his eyes, "Why is this man still alive?"

"Only thing trickier than a hungry judge, I figured, was bound to be a hungry governor. Therefore, I said, "Sirs, Your Honor. Your Honorable. Mister Neeley's attorney Mister Johnson accompanied us back to town from the location of their refreshment, and Mister Neeley's apprehension, to insure no harm befell the suspect while in our company."

"Did he now?" Governor Bigler asked.

"Bigler was a good man. Always spoke to all the fellows as if he was one with them. Smart son of a bitch too. No messing around with the lie or the liar for our Honorable Governor Bigler.

"Is this true Mister Johnson?" Bigler asked Neeley's attorney.

"Yes sir it is. I have been retained by Mister Neeley's father to assure that in all matters of legal import, the younger Mister Neeley is represented to the fullest and utmost letter of this great Union's legal code and I -"

"Shoot them both," Governor Bigler interrupted.

That shut Johnson up.

"Sir?" I asked.

"We have a state to build. We will not pander to every imbecile and bastard who lives among us."

Judge Parson looked at me, and Lucas Pritchard, and spat.

"You ever find as guilty a man as this one and waste my time with the prospect of a trial and the ramifications, legal, moral and emotional for the family the man has destroyed and I will have you both run out of the state. Understand me, sirs?"

We nodded.

Lucas asked, "Sirs, will we have to pay to bury them?"

"No."

The Judge continued, "Shoot them both unless Mister Johnson wants to step down as Mister Neeley's council. We can all go to dinner right after I return from my chambers where I shall inform the Popes, whom we just left in a whirl of emotion I could not begin to describe, that the man who decimated their lives and the life of their family has been brought to a rapid and lasting justice.

"I step down," Mister Johnson squeaked quickly.

I shot Latham Neeley in the belly as he opened his rotten mouth to speak. His body crumpled there on the walk. In front of the state capital. I shot him two more times. The man's warm blood splattered each of us.

I turned my gun on Mister Johnson and asked Governor Bigler, as he began wiping his face with his crisp white pocket-handkerchief, "You all want me to kill this son of a bitch? I got three more bullets."

As Mister Johnson pissed himself, Governor Bigler cringed.

"No Finney. It looks as though the counselor may be of a mind to choose future clients with a touch more care."

"Later when Johnson was elected Governor I sent him a wire congratulating him on his latest and wisest choice of client. We became friends. Later I told him I was glad, after all, I did not end up having to shoot him when I shot that other fellow."

Margie studied Finney. She knew some memories

haunted him more than others.

"Where is that boy?" she asked. "You must have told me that story a hundred times if you've told me once. I do not know if you are feeling well. Maybe some bitters would help."

Margie McCurren was Finney's fourth and youngest wife. She possessed an old and open soul but few people were as old and open as Finney McCurren. They met in the bank Finney owned on Market Street. At the young age of twenty-eight, she was a widowed and wealthy socialite. Her husband had been in sugar. A heart attack on a ship taking him to inspect plantations in South America the year before took him from her.

Margie knew Finney McCurren from parties and other social and charitable events. She knew he was one of the old timers raised, as a boy, in the hills of the gold country when California was in her infancy. The term Forty-niner never occurred to her until today.

Maybe it occurred to her because he spoke of the gold taken from the hills. Something Finney never spoke of with anyone except his son Laurence and Lucas's son James Pritchard. That Finney did take gold from the hills, a considerable amount of gold too, and not lost his life or his sanity was a commendable feat. The stories of the men and women crazy with the fever for treasure were not exaggerations. Margie's own father was a legislator for the state and used to tell his daughters of the madness in Sacramento. Her father introduced her to the sugar baron.

He later insisted she bank with Finney McCurren, "Because he, my dear, knows the awful value and power of money and what it can really do in our world."

Her beauty and exceptionally keen personality made

her a favorite at McCurren's.

"Here he is now. Good morning young fellow. Strong and hot and black. Margie made some camp coffee and it was tasty, but if you make more we'll drink it."

Finney placed his mug on the bar next to Margie's.

"Yes Sir Mister McCurren. Sorry I'm late, I encountered a bit of distraction in the supply car."

The barman was in his shirtsleeves and a woman's rouge was on his neck.

"Nothing to fret about my boy. Nothing at all. My young Missus and I were just discussing all the mad passionate nights I have kept her awake since we up and married last month. Weren't we darling?"

Margie leaned in, "The sooner you make that coffee the sooner we'll retire to the back of the train to talk to the deputy U.S. Marshal there. Make us an extra cup for him would you please?"

"Yes ma'am."

"And maybe a quick plate of ham and eggs for the boy too," Finney added.

"Yes sir."

"Where are we, do you know, son?"

The barman peered out either side of the dark train and at his pocket watch.

"We should be coming into San Jose station in a short while, at five this morning."

"Well that's fine; we'll be home for supper. Can you get someone to wire ahead for me to confirm our people know we will be arriving on time?"

The barman nodded and flipped eggs on a small sputtering griddle, "Yes sir, Mister McCurren, I sure can."

Finney and Margie held trays of steaming coffee with

stacks of hard fried eggs and circles of fried ham. Finney picked at the greasy ham with his fingers and chewed while they walked. Fat dribbled down his chin.

He whispered to Margie as they braced themselves from seat row to seat row, "Only thing tastes better than a fresh strong cup of coffee in the morning is a fresh strong cup of coffee with eggs fried in renderings. Yum."

The second to the last car of the train was a coach car with a smattering of passengers. Most were asleep, stretched out on empty bench seats. Snoring reverberated. Many an arm was flung over tired eyes. The train rocked its passengers to sleep as it sped up the state. In the last row, the McCurren's spied their new friend, deputy Doolen. He was awake and peering out the large black window at the dimness of a cool and clear California morning. The land flew past, slightly lit by the waning crescent moon.

"Deputy, we bring you breakfast and fresh coffee." Margie and Finney placed their trays on the benches around deputy Doolen and took a seat, handing him a steaming ceramic white mug. Deputy Doolen was tall and heavy, his eyes were dark, and his pockmarked face drooped with exhaustion. His large boots stood on the wooden floor next to his sore feet and he cradled a shotgun made of dark blue steel across his lap. Setting the shotgun aside, he rose slightly and took the proffered plate of steaming egg and ham from Missus McCurren.

"Thank you ma'am, Thank you Finney. Thank you very much."

Finney sat across the aisle and asked, "So how's this prisoner of yours doing, any trouble in the night?"

The deputy picked a hair from an egg and began to eat.

Mouth full he said, “Pardon me, I am powerful hungry.”

Finney waved him on.

“Yes sir. Lot of trouble. He cusses and hollers a lot, most other third class passengers been relocated to other cars. Mean son of a bitch he is. Won't stop the cussin' no matter what I do and then, whilst I was a catching a quick nap he took and pissed on all the seats he could reach where other passengers still was at. I hosed him down. That shut him up for a while but I dread the next few hours. Any notion how long 'til we're back in the city, sir?”

“Barman tells us we pull into San Jose in about fifteen minutes, at five this morning. We take on water and passengers and then it's another two hours to the city and the downtown terminal building. Your fellows know to meet you?”

“Yes sir.”

Finney crossed and picked the man's shotgun up off his lap.

“Why don't you take a moment to relieve yourself and we'll watch your prisoner. I'll make sure no one goes near him. How's that sound?”

“I can't let him out of my sight, that's my orders.”

“I won't let him shoot your prisoner. He'll be fine for a moment without you,” Margie said.

Doolen acquiesced and pulled on his boots, squared his hat on his head. In a moment, he stepped out the back of the car.

Margie asked Finney, “What did this man do? Why is he being brought back to the city?”

“That is Bob Tanner. Bob Tanner is a wanted bank robber, among other things. He had an exceptional run in San

Francisco two months ago. He and his brother took a lot of money from a lot of people. A few of my friends and I sent Pinkertons after the Tanner Brothers but the law found them first. Pity, those Pinkertons have a propensity toward finishing business which reminds me of a younger me."

"Undoubtedly you get what you pay money for. Was anything stolen recovered?"

"No," Finney smiled, "not yet."

"Any trouble?" The deputy swung back into his seat as Finney handed the shotgun to him.

"None at all."

"He never stirred. Nice weapon. State issue?"

"No sir. This one's mine."

"Okay deputy, eat up and we'll check on you after we pull out of the San Jose station."

Chapter Eight

In their private car, the McCurren's read the papers from the day before and spent time working over balance sheets, checking totals in long addition.

Finney looked over at Margie, "My pretty little banker, who suspected you owned such a fine head for numbers. If your late husband realized your worth as a mathematician I wager you would have been on that ship with him when he suffered his attack."

Margie squeezed his hand.

"When I die I want you to promise you'll only remarry a man with more money than you. It's the only safe choice for a woman of means these days. When I think of how much wealthier you are than I am with my banks and my investments and the properties I own, it makes me a little frisky."

Margie threw her head back and laughed.

"The wind blowing and birds singing makes you frisky Finney McCurren. To my knowledge the word "little" has not entered the equation yet."

She continued to hold his hand.

"Who other than my late husband and a rare handful of commodities brokers knew sugar, in so many forms, would be so profitable to buy and sell? I never guessed what poor Horace was worth. I did not believe it until I touched the deed and bond on every investment. Visiting my farms and plantations is a brilliant idea for a honeymoon. Meeting you will help put a bit more jump in people's pants when I tell them what I want and how I want it. It is hard to kick ass when you are woman. No one thinks you'll do it until they meet you or someone whose ass you already kicked."

Finney brightened at her talk of asses. She was a

remarkable woman.

Margie smiled with anticipation.

"I can't wait to see your family again and give them all the fine things we bought for the children. I'm so pleased they like me."

She paused.

"My being younger than your son was strange at first, but everyone has so much love and respect for you I think you could have married an Amazonian monkey and they would have fallen all over themselves to make sure you were happy."

Finney laughed, "I can't hide having your own means eased the apprehension over your age. You are older beyond your years. Wealth does that to a woman on her own. I've seen it in other women at the bank. I'd have laid into them all until they treated you right if they had not warmed to you naturally. Of course, that was unnecessary. Poor Caroline and I raised the boy right, and he has a fine family."

Returning papers to their rightful places, "We're slowing. We must be approaching the station."

San Jose station rose before the train. Large and granite, clean and deserted save the few men and women waiting to get an early jump to the city. As they slowed, the train made a few gentle lurches. A knock came at the door. Finney stood and unlocked the brass latch on the walnut door and the tall pale porter entered their private car.

"Sir, madam, they are telling us there has been quite a lot of earthquake activity this morning, to the point where debris or perhaps some small damage affected the tracks ahead. We may be here for some time while we wait for work crews to send word back on the status of the tracks. Is there anything either of you require."

Finney resumed his seat on the overstuffed divan, "Okay Wilson, just let us know when the situation changes and have the barman send more fresh coffee please."

"Yes sir," Wilson bowed and turned.

A moment later Margie opened the door to the passage and stood looking out the many windows across numerous pairs of tracks far opposite them, to the open side of a still train. She scanned the ground but found nothing unusual to note, "I suspected nothing, no idea. Amazing, we're speeding along faster than anything on land and quakes shook hard enough to perhaps damage the tracks."

"I ever tell you about the quake of eighteen sixty eight?" Finney called to her.

"Wednesday, October twenty first, eighteen sixty eight. I can feel it like it is right now. Just before eight in the morning. On a glorious morning. We were in bed, Caroline, Laurence and I. Laurence was asleep. We were snuggled up, you know, as young married people are apt to do when the baby is sleeping and no one needs to be anywhere too early. We were in the new house on Buena Vista Avenue.

"We could hear the help downstairs finishing with the breakfast preparation. My valet had been shuffling about on the other side of my dressing room door for a while. Caroline sent the nurse away to the nursery because the baby was asleep and happy. The three of us were snuggled in bed, warm, cozy. The sun shone through the eastern windows and lit the entire room. I remember, Caroline told me she wanted me to spoon her. I told her I'd rather fork her. Ha-ha. Get me? Fork?

Margie, now sitting across from the old man slapped his knee, "I get you. Not much to get you old coot."

Finney smiled, continued, "At first we didn't know

what was happening. Each of us though the other was shaking the bed. Then we knew and we lay there in that feather bed, the three of us together. It did not matter if the house collapsed. If we never saw anyone else again. We were together and suddenly expected to die together."

He stared at the station.

"You know how quakes are. Little one's are a bit of an inconvenience so long as nothing moves too much or falls on you. The medium one's scare a fellow but are still a lark so long as no one gets hurt its okay.

"But the big one. That is what we all called it. The big one of sixty-eight. It scared the bejeezus out of us. Wardrobes opened their doors and dumped our clothes. Chests of drawers slid away from walls and tumbled, crashing open. Chairs and stools literally jumped across the room while vases and shelf treasures, souvenirs and the like, fell off, leaped off, and smashed.

"Neither of us screamed although we could hear Cook, fat Missus Patty, and Melody, the maid with the wandering eye, hollering all the way from outside where they either ran or had been sharing a quiet moment. The three of us lay silently. The baby nestled up with Caroline. Caroline warm in my arms. We were terrified, while at peace. I closed my eyes as the bed traveled across the room. Bits of plaster fell in chunks from the ceiling and the front wall.

"Not much damage compared to the rest of the city. That's why we built on the hills. Lucas told me "You carve your foundations out of stone and you won't be carving your house out of rubble when the quakes subside."

"He was right. It ended. Neither of us said a word. The clocks stopped in our bedroom, in all the rooms through the house. Apparently pendulums get confused which way to tick and tock during the vibrations. Next thing we know all the help, the entire household, burst into the room from the doors they used most often, almost all at once and together.

"Even Ned the stable boy was in there with us. They were scared and staring at us, still in bed. Rob, the driver, still in his skivvies. I sent them all off to get fully dressed and instructed each to arm themselves. Only a matter of time until the worse off came to check on the folks at the top of the hill. Happens every time. They cooked food and bread easily served outside in front of the house. Cook carried a butcher knife in her apron for a month.

"I received word from the bank they were okay downtown. Minor structural damage. The streets filled with worried citizens. We sent for extra Pinkertons to secure executive houses and the bank. People did fret. Not violently but many a distraught citizen was observed walking about in distracted disbelief that day. A Wednesday not many who were alive will ever forget.

As they sat in their private car looking out the window at the few people on the platform they both felt the train begin to move.

"I guess they received the all clear," Margie said.

Then they stopped moving.

The people on the platform showed silent signs of surprise. The train lurched again but this time rocked from side to side as though blindsided by another locomotive. They heard crashing and great cracking and jumped to their feet as the people on the platform ran and one entire end of the station collapsed in a thick plume of dust. They watched men and women collapse in the rubble, they heard their injured cries. The train continued to rock so violently it threw each down while tables and crockery, books and bits of travel luggage showered upon them.

They heard the screams of fellow passengers and rapid footfalls down the passage outside their closed doors. The shaking continued and horrifying crashes sounded all around as Finney lunged to the door and slid the brass bolts home. He crawled to the heavy black worn leather satchel on the divan near where he had sat and pulled out a very long and very clean bluish gray revolver. Popping the chamber open, he checked his bullets. Closing the chamber with a smart slap on the palm of his left hand, he located and pocketed a box of rounds in an empty jacket pocket.

Crawling he returned to his speechless bride who was now on her knees watching slices of San Jose crumble no more than a few hundred yards away. Debris rolled across the platform toward their car. He pulled her back down to the floor just as a wave of water burst violently against the car's wall shattering some windows and washed over the forward most cars of the train. The station's water tower fell and nearly washed their section of the train off the tracks. They felt the great car lift, saw gaps of light where highly polished walnut planks briefly separated, lurched as the car tilted, and slammed back onto hard ground.

Water ran down the unbroken windows and the station was gone. Rubble was everywhere. Suddenly they were wet and smelled natural gas.

Sprawled on thick damp carpets littered with wet sand and shards of glass, Finney spoke sternly, “We run now. Grab one bag, anything right here now handy and we are out this door.”

He pointed at the door behind them.

“You stay close to me. If I shoot anyone, you do not fret. You hear me?”

Margie slightly bit her bottom lip, nodded.

"Yes? Good. We need to check on the deputy."

He slid the brass bolts. There was no one in the passage. His gun down, they entered the passage and ran to the end of the car. Out the end door and onto the car's landing their quick steps clanked as they descended metal stairs and he jumped to the damp ground avoiding the shambled platform. Turning, Finney helped Margie leap from the lowest metal stair.

Finney noticed the car no longer sat on the tracks. The water violently derailed the front cars but placed them gingerly down a few inches off and parallel to the tracks.

The ground moved, more buildings in San Jose shook and fell. Screams and the sound of the earth shuddering were so loud they hurt the nerves in Finney's ears and teeth. He grabbed her bag up with his, clasped Margie's hand and ran with her to the furthest spot in the yard. An errant boxcar lumbered along an empty track before them. It kept on rolling and they heard it crash to a stop against another stationary uncoupled car.

They stopped and lay down in brown grass where no loose trains could run them over and no building or signal poles could fall on them. Margie lay with the satchel bags under her arms. Finney rested the large revolver between them. He rolled onto his back as he fished a pewter flask from a pocket in his suit vest. Unscrewing the small lid, he offered the little metal bottle to Margie who took it greedily and drank half the contents in one burning pull.

She burped, tears watered in her eyes, and handed it back. He took one short stinging swallows.

"Now what?" She looked at him, looked at the destruction of the station, looked at the large revolver.

Distant explosions began to tear through town. People streamed out of the train onto the platform and into the roads going nowhere as quickly as they could.

"Now we watch them fret. Now we figure how to get to the city as quickly as we can. We steal or buy horses. That's to be the only way I wager. I think it's still going. You feel it?"

"I do. It's been at least fifty seconds."

"And there's bound to be after quakes for a while to come. Anything on that train you can't live without?"

"A rare bottle of Rye for Laurence. My clothes. No. All my papers are in here and I have you. Let's go."

Finney grimaced, "I got a badge in that damn trunk in our car. I ain't running back in for the star that never protected me when I was a deputy U.S. Marshal. Getting blowed up over an old memory would be pretty damn stupid."

Margie whispered, "My jewelry. The cameos. The one from your mother, the ones from my grandmother, and the ones you've given me."

"Damn," Finney muttered.

"They're in the lockbox in the green and blue trunk in the back," Margie began to rise.

Finney grabbed her heavy red skirt and gently yanked her to the ground.

"What we're gonna need is rifles and more guns and two horses, four would be better. Are there horses on the train?"

Margie watched him think and knew staying down was what he meant by not fretting.

Ignoring the screaming inside her she spoke, evenly, calmly, "I don't think so. We can go look before the rest of them start thinking what we're thinking."

"Let's go," he grabbed the revolver and two bags.

They walked back to the train and down its length to the livestock cars. In the second, they spied through wooden slats six fine, agitated, pleasure horses.

"If we can get them out of here without shooting anyone it'll be dandy. We start shooting and everyone else will start shooting. We'll have the damn National Guard here sooner than anyone wants, we don't need to fuss with them. Be enough fuss when we get to the city, I reckon. If we get the deputy to come with us, his badge might make things easier than harder. You get in this car and pick the four best horses, six if they're as fine as they look from here and I'll fetch deputy Doolen."

Margie hoisted herself up and in after they managed to slightly open the rolling door to the livestock car. Hefting their satchels in after, he pushed and she pulled the heavy door shut.

"You start feeling woozy get on over to where we were watching from and I'll find you. I ain't back by the time the sun rises clear you go on without me. Find a gun and ride like hell to the city. Take strange ways you know won't be heavily peopled. Maybe cut over to Merced and get onto the beach north of Fort Funston and back into town through the Park?"

She gave him a peck through the slats and off he walked. He crouched in the twilight and skirted down the long row of cars. She turned to face the horses and began speaking to them in low soft soothing tones.

At the second to last car, Finney heard the shouting he dreaded. Deputy Doolen yelled at the civilians to leave the train and run. The man chained all night to the pipe in the wall told him what to say.

The smell of natural gas was stronger at the rear of the train. Finney reasoned a main near the station must have cracked. How long until it ignited? How big a flame cloud, he wondered. He had seen gas clouds erupt into flame before. In the mountains in the mines, they were a rolling roiling terror. Off in town he noticed little fires starting and knew the gas and the entire train did not have long. Slipping the large gun into a trouser pocket, he pulled a small knife from his belt. The blade was no longer than his middle finger.

He snuck around quickly to the end of the car. He jumped and lifted himself onto the stairs without a sound. His hand found the latch to the door and slid it back slowly. He slipped inside, silently closed the door again. He heard a mumbling and a sound like a strained whimper.

Squatting low and removing his hat Finney poked his head around the edge of the rear bulkhead. In the last row of seats, where earlier the deputy drank coffee and ate fried eggs with the McCurrens, the manacled man's arm, up to his elbow, lay on the floor still chained to the pipe. His flailing stump was bandaged with what looked like an old lady's black shawl.

The deputy's gun was in the man's remaining hand. He pointed at the frightened deputy who was doing his best to tie a tourniquet around the prisoner's bleeding and waving stump.

"I liked my damned arm. I liked it a helluva lot! When you're done tying that off your gonna give me my damned arm off the damned floor. Then I'm a gonna chain you to the damned train and kick you 'til your damned arm rips off too."

Before either knew what happened Finney was on top of the man with one arm stabbing him in the soft of his neck while punching him in his stump. The deputy's gun was pinned beneath Finney's leg, grasped by lifeless fingers against the man's chest.

"Get the gun!" Finney yelled, "You smell the gas! If it fires, we're dead! Get your gun!"

The deputy reached around and slid the gun from the quaking fingers of the dead man's hand.

"Got it."

"Good, let's go. Get your kit. Were riding to the city but have to get out of this gas cloud as fast as we can. Bring your shotgun. Make sure the safeties are on."

Finney asked, "You have any more guns than these two?"

"Two more in my bag, man in the caboose has a rifle he targets with when they're running through the desert, I'll get it."

Finney told him as they exited the car, "I left Margie alone four cars up, livestock car, get your kit and the rifle and all the shells you can carry and meet us up there. We have to go now. San Jose is gone and if we don't get out now we'll all be stuck here for a week. Ever spend a week in San Jose? I have. The earthquake may improve things a tad but we still need to be in the city."

Finney skirted back down the line of cars avoiding people as much as he could.

As he passed the livestock car, he peaked in and whispered, "Be ready, one minute or two more, deputy is fine and will join you here shortly."

He ran off before she replied or asked him what happened or where he was going. The gasps of disbelief the screams of panic were now palpable. The smell was getting stronger. It was a matter of minutes until the entire train yard became a blaze of death and destruction. He found their private car at the front of the line and snuck back up the steps.

Knife hidden, he entered the passage and then their car. Things were worse than he remembered. Their possessions were all over the car. Strewn about the car were clothes that he recognized as Margie's and his own, someone had picked over the bottles on the bar. He recognized and pocketed the untouched Rye. A tink, tink, sound from the sleeping area at the rear of the car caught his attention. Peering in he spied a man in a brown coat attempting to work the blade of a clasp knife into the crack between the lid and the body of the strong box just removed from the green and blue steamer trunk.

Jumping as he had in the rear car Finney plunged his little knife into the side of the man's neck before he even turned to see who was stabbing him. Finney pulled his knife out and the man's neck started pulsing warm blood. His big limp body slipped off the end of the bed and landed on the floor. Grabbing up the clasp knife and strongbox Finney started back out to the passage. Checking carefully he slowly made his way back out and down the metal stairs. He gagged on the odor of gas as his boots squelched into the soggy earth.

Sprinting as quickly as a tired old man could he returned to the livestock car in time to find a man pulling the deputy out of the car by his belt onto the ground. Door wide, Margie grabbed the handle, mustered her strength, and rolled its weight onto the stranger's head as he grabbed at her mud-tinged skirts. Wailing in agony, head pinned, Margie kicked the man in the face with her lace up boots as Finney stabbed him in the ribs with the stolen clasp knife.

"Open the door Margie," Finney said, "he's dead."

She opened the door and the man's body slipped and collapsed to the ground.

"Climb up," She said wiping her hands on her skirts.

Finney handed up the strong box and the deputy's pack. Taking the knife from the man's side Finney helped the tired deputy to his feet and then scrambled into the car and up onto one of the saddled horses.

"We're leaving, where's that rifle, son?" Finney asked the deputy.

He found Finney's hat and tossed it and then the rifle into waiting hands. Finney placed one on his head and chambered a round in the other. The deputy climbed up into the car and found a horse with a braided rope bridle and worn saddle.

Margie said, "We have to take them out on the platform side, there's no ramp and the car isn't wide enough to jump them out."

She rolled back the platform door. Finney rode out with two horses in tow, the strong box secured by Margie to the back of the last. He swung his long Colt about him in show, safety on, rifle across his lap. Margie mounted and followed, the deputy trailed after. They rode the length of the platform; each jumped their horse off the end and turned to follow the tracks away from San Jose to the city.

Riding ahead Finney stopped, collected and secured their black portmanteaus and remounted by the time the Margie and the deputy caught up. They passed him and he chased them, all speeding flat out as quickly as each horse could gallop. When they were over a rifle shot away from the demolished platform they slowed to a fast trot and rode three abreast, Margie in the middle.

The wind that whooshed past their faces and around

their ears increased the moment before the loudest noise any of them had ever heard imploded behind as the ground and the sky lit in a single instance of burning horror.

Looking back over his shoulder the deputy saw the massive fireball rise into the sky. They stopped and each watched the distant tragedy.

Finney asked the deputy, "How'd that man's arm come to be cut off so clean?"

"He was sitting with the window open and his elbow resting on the sash. When the quakes hit the window slammed shut and the brittle wood gave way to the heavy pane of glass. Took his entire elbow right off. I seen the elbow piece when I was outside the car after I got the rifle. It was a clean cut."

"Who was that fellow I stabbed in the ribs at the livestock car?"

"The man who owned that rifle."

"Huh. Suppose it must be a good one then."

Marge told them, "I was thinking about how to get to the city while I saddled the horses. The main roads will fill with people leaving San Francisco if the damage there is as great as here. What if we continue up the peninsula on these rails? The horses will find plenty to graze on and there is bound to be water. No trains will be heading up behind us; we know that for sure. It will be rather stealthy. No one will be waiting for their train and if they are we can certainly out run them if they attempt to chase us."

Finney added, "And we can enter the city in the center but close enough to downtown to look in on things and then skirt up the hills to the house on Buena Vista Avenue. If it's a mess, we can cut to the ocean and then back into town through the Golden Gate Park. Brilliant my dear, brilliant.

Chapter Nine

I walked away from the rolling plumes of smoke and my father and the men who fought to control the tragedy that threatened to engulf our entire city. In the distance, over the bellow of the blaze, I heard the sound of explosions. Dynamite detonated with the intention to slow the fires and contain the devastation.

My trek back to the location where James left me was fast. Return trips are always faster, I reflected, than going somewhere. I thought of the first time my family crossed the bay to our friend's estate in Sausalito. The ride on the small sailboat was cold and fun. The captain, my Godfather James Pritchard, tacked, turned, entertained the children, and startled the mothers and servants.

Laurence and James stood at the prow with cigars smoldering in their clenched jaws. The entire company stared in awe at the sun and the fog lighting our city in majestic profile. From the low point on the water's surface, the entire Pacific Ocean beneath us, and the beauty of the city in the distance, I felt proud of being a small part of a large world. The anticipation of the shore and the tracts of undisturbed grassy land to romp about kept my brother's eyes looking toward the coming North.

Two days later, we were satisfied. A fine time enjoyed by all ended. We fished, sailed, played games, and ate. The grownups told scary stories by the dancing light of driftwood fires. We boys slept in an idiot pile of blankets and jammies and pillows. The return in the little boat and the anticipation of return to one's own room and life was as enticing as the lure of the unknown shore had been.

I thought at that time the jaunt back to the city took the same amount of time, perhaps longer due to a wind trying to blow the boat back where we departed. In my mind the return home, the return to familiarity and routine was the blink of an eye compared to the long jump into the excitement of weekend adventure.

I skirted the area where I left Father Augustine. Recalled the oath recited earlier with James Pritchard and I fingered the worn badge in my pocket. How did being a deputy, if I was in fact a deputy and not a dupe, and an oath to uphold the laws of my state reconcile the demands of Judicious Theology, a priest, and a God who seemed larger than a municipality?

As I traversed a mountain of rubble and the hazards of broken glass, sharp spears of timber, and footholds that gave away suddenly in the dust, I looked up at the building next. I was high enough on the pile of debris to be higher than second floor windows. The building nearby was a tenement. The rooms were dark and appeared to be empty behind smashed windows.

As I picked my way over a precarious fall of brick, I heard moaning, stopped and listened. Moaning came from a window so close I could have jumped onto the sill. I looked from the broken panes deeper into the room. On a disheveled bed were two people. Naked, a man's bare bottom bobbed on the bed while a woman's legs splayed, jerked, and rocked, clasp, and unclasp the man's backside. Her knees rose and fell with rhythm as the man's movement became hurried.

As their bodies surged together, one of the woman's hands reached up and over and felt about atop an old disheveled nightstand. The hand located a brown pocketbook. The other hand came up over the man's head; his face was lost in long swirls of auburn hair and stained pillows. She moaned louder and opened the pocket book and extracted paper bills. One arm reached and found a rip in the striped mattress ticking where cotton wool was exposed.

She silently stuffed the bills into the tear as her moans increased in volume. The woman's legs scissored and locked around the man's puckered pale bottom. Her arms met above the sweaty baldhead again and replaced the pocket book gingerly on the nightstand. His moans and her exclamations of pleasure reached a point of no return. His bottom tightened and his toes curled in soiled, bedraggled bedclothes. I noticed my own erection. As the woman giggled with girlish pleasure and rolled on top of the sweaty bald man, she spied me on the mountain outside her window.

Our eyes met. Her areolas were like large round circles of chocolate covering the entire tip of each soft and stretched pale breast. She slowly lowered them onto the man's face, obstructing his sight. She placed a finger to her parted, moaning lips and winked at me. She sat up and pulled a worn counterpane from the other side of the thin mattress over their nakedness, and their heads. A writhing mound of fabric, they were lost from sight. I resumed descent while the pressure of arousal subsided. Once on the pavement I again made the way stealthily back to the outskirts of the disaster.

I found James Pritchard standing in a circle of other men. They spoke of the destruction each witnessed.

As I approached James said, "Here he is, none too soon. I trust you located the Lieutenant without trouble."

"I did," was my weak reply. "He has requests."

"Of course he has." The needs of Laurence's men made plane, James spoke to the necessary volunteers to get all required into placc as quickly as possible.

"We need to get across the bay. I fear how long it may take us to get across town. The rumors of armed gangs are growing. As are the accounts of armed vigilantes settling accounts, new and old. The last thing either of us needs is trouble on a day when every man has a legal right to be armed."

James walked me to the automobile.

"We'll stop by the Green Hag on Haight for a fast business then make our way to Sausalito. There we can relax. A cold swim, a hot bath, and a full night's sleep. With no more tremors. Sound good?"

"Sounds too good to be true."

Chapter Ten

Sausalito was boring. The water was fun and the food was good, but their mother and auntie sat and drank wine and talked until the baby was asleep so the two little boys decided they had nothing left to do. Sean fell asleep for a nap. He curled up in the bed his mother and father slept in when visiting the Sausalito estate but Aidan was not tired. He missed his house, he missed his father, and he missed his big brother. He pulled on his jacket and walked down to the water's edge, found the men loading the boat and hopped aboard.

With a bump, the craft pulled out from the pier. Down below, he soon felt the familiar rocking; the lazy lapping of the waves on the motionless hull became a steady hum of water rushing by. He dozed for a moment and woke when the boat again bumped lazily against the pier. He snuck his little head up to the deck and saw the way was clear. Down the deck and jumped to the pier, he ran up more ramps and made his way around seagull poop and crusty old looking sailors engulfed in massive, stinking nets.

The first teamster he saw headed south he followed. When the wagon slowed a little, Aidan, no more than eight and wearing short pants with a thick sweater and a blue duffle coat, leaped onto the back, climbed aboard, and burrowed into crates and loose straw. The wagon was slow and stopped often. Police officers and angry looking men on horseback with long rifles or thick shotguns lingered on every corner. Small fires were kept blazing in intersections, debris being burned in a controlled manner while men warmed themselves. Aidan recognized occasional landmarks on Divisadero Street. Many were missing. He counted the blocks and read the signs that still stood.

When they approached the hill and he recognized more street signs, Aidan slid to the rear of the wagon, dangled his legs, and leaped. He ran with momentum until he could slow without stumbling and falling. Climbing the hills, he soon saw his house and his park. The gaslights were off and he was hungry. More men stood around the house and the neighbor's houses. They too had guns. They too warmed themselves with small fires in the center of the street. He was hungry but thought sneaking into his own house might get him caught or killed. Then he thought of the butcher's shop.

Every morning his mother walked down the park to Haight Street. She visited the butcher's shop, the Steak and Egger, and always returned with a chop for each of them for breakfast and fresh eggs. He accompanied her a few times and remembered the long strings of sausages kept about the counter just out of reach of the ugly butcher's ugly dog.

"Surely, they would give me a sausage or two on mother's account," he thought to himself as he began walking down the hill through the park, hands thrust in pockets.

The sun had almost set. He needed to hurry to make it to the shop before closing. He leapt tree trunks and ran past people who heard him but did not see him in the underbrush. At the bottom of the hill, he kept to the side streets and calculated the shortest distance to the front of the Steak and Egger.

He need not have worried. No one was interested in what a single small boy was about. Gangs of men stood in the center of Haight Street. Many more had guns and were starting small fires. Aidan did not recognize the men or see any of the police officers who usually wore blue uniforms and rode on very large dark horses. Some of the men sang, others clutched women and were crying. Most were, it appeared, headed to the Avenue Drive. They had ridden past there earlier, his brother, sister, mother, and he. Aidan and Sean decided they despised the little park. Most of the people in the Avenue Drive were sad and messy.

He spied the sign for the butcher's shop. The butcher was standing in front. He looked angry. Men approached his shop and he spoke to them. First, the butcher spoke to them like customers. He raised his large bushy eyebrows in a question and smiled. Whatever the men said he did not like so he crossed his arms and frowned. The men spoke to the butcher again; he shook his head and held up his palms.

They did not notice Aidan approach. They did not notice him step onto the store's stoop and enter. No one saw him in the shop. The butcher started yelling at the men in a language Aidan did not understand. He spied the hard sausages. They were like beautiful ropes of red marble tied together and draped lovingly over the top of the wooden counter. He reached out and grabbed the shortest string. It had only two sausages. He grabbed another of only two. He stuffed them into each duffle coat pocket.

One of the men the butcher was arguing with yelled, "At-a boy, ha-ha Sam, you cheap old bastard!"

Aidan turned and saw the three men filling the door. He saw the butcher turn and heard the butcher yell. Before he knew what he was doing, Aidan ran the length of the counter and pushed through a rear-whitewashed door. He heard the butcher running after him, then he heard him stop, shut and lock his front door. Aidan was in the back of the shop. It stank like putrid meats and had slicks of red liquid all over the cold hard floors. He turned and saw a back door with faint sunlight filtering in around the edges where it failed to shut completely.

He was through the door and into an area common to all the shops divided by rickety wooden fences. He ran past pins of different stinking animals and heard the sound of the butcher's dog being shoved out the door he had just slammed shut. Up a stand of shipping crates, Aidan was over the fence in one fast leap. He landed in a puddle of muddy water. He was up and on his feet as quick as a cat.

The boy darted down filthy wet cobbled streets. He was fast and small. His little legs pumped, jumping curbs, dodging horse pies. His scrawny arms flailed keeping him balanced and upright as breath came faster into little lungs that filled and emptied like grain sacks that would eventually burst. In two blocks sweat dripped down his face leaving little pale clean paths where the dirt had been and little smears of clean when he wiped the sweat away with his now filthy sleeve.

He ran toward the safety of the dark hill-covered park across from his house but started in the wrong direction. Air that usually smelled like horse dung and motor exhaust and old wash water now stank like a char pit, hazy with ash and smoke and soot. He clenched his cap in one hand as he turned his little head and quickly stole a glance behind him. The dog was still there.

Whip-fast, brown, and white with wiry short hair, the muscled dog, not much smaller than Aidan, was accustomed to catching rats and varmints in the shrubbery that lined most of the cities nicer parks. The dog did not snarl so much as pant with a growl, "harg, harg, harg." A white patch like a rich man's cravat covered the dog's neck and chest. Aidan recognized the mutt from his trips to the butcher's shop with his mother. He had never noticed the stain before, the white patch stained pink with the blood of small animals and, Aidan now thought as he ran for his life, little boys with pockets full of marbled-red sausages. Rodents and small animals snatched from greasy dustbins and little boys, flung about the gutter until dead, and broken enough for champing up for an always-hungry dog's supper.

Aidan ran past a clutch of crying women holding two little broken bodies. An ashy old granny on her hands and knees, dressed in black, picked through rubble for an empty little black boot that once shone like sun light on calm water. He knew those moms and aunties. That was the Fenner twin's family. Those are the Fenner twins, Tad and Tan. Are they dead? The old woman, on her knees, raised her head from the task of dumping sand out of and polishing the small black leather boot. She looked at him. Blood and spittle dribbled from her mouth to her chin and heavy tears silently rolled down her sunken old cheeks.

As Aidan rounded the next corner onto Waller Street, he dumped a pocket of stolen sausages and sprinted. The dog skidded around the corner and was on the meat in an instant, the "harg, harg, harg," replaced by hard greedy gulping as Aidan rounded another corner onto lower Buena Vista Avenue West. Up the street and past a stoop he stopped, dropped to his side, and, lifting cracked batten siding, rolled into a gap enclosing him in damp earth and dry sticky cobwebs.

Aidan laid still. His heart raced. He felt its beat in his neck, eyes, and ears. His little body shook with the cold of the damp earth and his exhausting effort first to escape his pursuers and now to calm himself. He quietly gulped breath the way the dog had gulped abandoned sausages. Over his heart and breathing Aidan strained to hear if his pursuer, the dog's master, was on Buena Vista Avenue yet.

"God damn little bastard," he heard.

Then a yelp and the sound of the dog kicked hard and the shock of the dog's body slamming against the buildings cracked siding where Aidan hid. He remembered the other sausages in his other jacket pocket and prayed the kicked dog missed the scent coming from beneath the house.

Another fierce kick and a yelp and the dog could not smell anything. Blood caked his nose. Hunched in a corner of garbage and crates the mutt distanced itself as far as possible from another abusing boot.

"God damn little bastard. If Schmitz says it's okay to shoot them then I'll load my bird rifle and settle a few scores."

To the dog he spit, "Useless mangy cur. Get your greedy hide out here. I ought a tie a brick to your neck or sell you to one of those butchers in the Chinatown, real cheap."

The dog left the protection of his nook and sped back down the street. The dog yelped again as the man gave him another boot in his filthy little rear.

Aidan heard the pair move back down the hill but he did not stir. He was cold, tired, and so hungry. He ate a hard sausage retrieved from his pocket. It was dry and chewy and tasted like metal. It was better than the smell of soot or the taste of ashes that coated his tongue.

The fat muttering butcher wiped his hands on his apron as he followed the dog down the middle of the slick ash-strewn street.

"I got shells. I got lots a' them shells. I can use the sheep and swine gun. I'll bang a drum and the little villains will come a running."

Chapter Eleven

The sky was a horror show of color. Fire glowed pink in the east beyond the silhouettes of the remaining dark buildings. Pink and orange faded up to a darkening blue sky darker than usual due to the fine floating ash. It fell from above and coated the wreckage in every neighborhood.

A breeze was picking up and blowing stronger from the west. It reddened cheeks and cracked lips and hands unless rubbed with lard. The reek of the fires mingled with the smell of the dead. Charred or unburned, runoff water from fire hoses and broken water mains bloated the bodies of unclaimed adults and children. Dead animals were too numerous to be disposed of quickly. Around every broken city block, dazed and broken survivors peer into the rubble and filth as if looking for the handholds to their old lives wrested from their grasp only hours earlier.

April was a pretty month in the city. Families picnicked in parks full of wild flowers made healthy and lush by winter rains. Easter Sunday was three days earlier. Now many churches were gone or partially destroyed and their parishioners had no thoughts of celebrating God. They each needed God's help. The shops full of bright pretty dresses and hats were gone. Women dyed their Easter dresses black in nineteen-o-six. Concerned citizens combed over the hulks of buildings helping one another in the desperate search for loved ones and prized possessions.

Bands of looters took to the streets in search of easy spoils, food and livestock. Likewise, armies of little boys and girls combed the mounds in pursuit of treasure or food. When they found an unstable, freestanding lurching wall, boys and girls rushed around the base while others hurled bricks and stones at the top, seeing whom it would flatten if they persuaded the stubborn masonry to release its grasp of ruined foundations.

Walking down Masonic Street, returning to his shop, the butcher spied his young wife in the center of Haight Street. Men and boys surrounded her. Their intentions were clear.

"Clarice, you know we won't tell Sam," one gangly youth said. A fine round white bare breast with the lightest pink areola and tiny taught nipple stood next to a taught string from her loosed bodice. The boy slowly wound the string around his finger. He used it, gently teasing her exposed nipple. His other hand was around her and planted firmly on the skirts that hid her shapely backside. She did not understand his words but she understood, liked the feel of him, them, warm and close to her. She felt the hot breath on her exposed breast.

The butcher saw the pup, the Mangy Mick touching his sweet Clarice. He walked quickly, dog at his heals, as he loosened from under his apron and palmed a ten-inch swine blade. Jumping thought the circle of men the butcher cut Clarice's bodice string lose from the froward youth by taking the fingers on his right hand cleanly off. Bits of the young man's hand spilled onto her tall lace-up black boots. The boots a moment ago she broke a heel off in a paving crack and caused her to lose her balance and trip into the arms of the boy whose fingers she now began curiously stepping gently on.

Clarice, used to blood in the butcher's shop, said nothing when it warmly spurted her free breast. The sound the boy made as he crumpled to the paving stones at her feet sounded faintly like a pig or a rabbit she had not quite finished killing in one of the filthy pins at the back of the shop or on her Papa's wasting farm. The boy's blood felt familiar.

She was not oblivious to the chop the butcher made into the soft front of the kneeling boy's neck. Her husband stood squarely above and behind him. The back and long tip of the blackened steel blade protruded from the boy's neck. The strength in the butcher's grasp on the blood-slick wooden handle was the only force keeping the gangly and slightly flinching body from crumpling completely at her feet.

Clarice giggled as she looked into the butcher's red face. People said she came to him from the old country to settle a debt owed by the butcher's uncle. She feared and loved the way his eyes looked into her when he was frustrated and angry. The circle of men and boys backed away and disappeared. This was not the first or last fool cut open by butcher Samaritan Fundenburg over his dimwitted young lovely bride.

The boy's body became filthy and dropped to the paving stones with a loud knock from his now thoughtless head. The girl's large blood-spattered breast, dress and boots held every man's stare. Young Clarice looked at the brutish Samaritan in a way that surprised them to a man. Over the smell and death and one boy's final pain she looked at her butcher like a fool excited by the realization of her power over a bigger fool.

He wiped the long knife clean on his apron and sheathed it underneath, next to his growing arousal. The butcher walked around the clumped body. He stood in the growing pool of blood as he reached with bloody hands to replace her breast and lace up his little bride. Again, he kicked at his dog, this time away from the dead boy's fingers Clarice rolled with the toe of one boot. As they walked to the butcher's shop, the boy's blood tracked after them from the soles of the butcher's boots. Men converged on the body. They stole its boots and other few possessions and dragged his carcass into the teeming gutter.

I was one of the admirers dispersed from Clarice's circle by the butcher's appearance and angry chops. I visited the butcher's wife more than once in the back of the shop while the butcher was on his wagon making deliveries. I was with her the night before the quake. I was about to assist Clarice and remove the boy from her undergarments when the butcher appeared in a rage on Haight Street. In my mind's eye I saw her naked. In my nostrils, I smelled her soft flowery scent. She smelled sweeter than the white silky powders at the barber's shop.

Clarice was being lead away. The night before, my trembling hands untied the strings of her bodice by candle light and removed the silk smalls she wore beneath her skirts. The butcher tied her bodice strings, her silky smalls, in red clotting knots. Knots cut later by the butcher in a private moment to release her from her binding skirts and lace.

It was I she bared her breast to in the middle of an ashy street teeming with the walking injured and shockingly bereaved. No one on that street of misery noticed her nakedness until the drunken toughs I grew up avoiding stumbled out of the Green Hag's Inn. Their drunken press broke her boot heel and separated us in a way the smashed and burned rubble of the city had been unable.

"It is your good fortune to be alive," James said from the door of the Green Hag.

In my mind's eye, I saw myself struck mute with the loss of fingers and my head nearly severed by a single vehement blow.

"If the drunken lads had not inadvertently stumbled onto Clarice's bold exposure, you might be dead. Or both you and Sam might be dead."

James clutched the handles of his small portmanteau in a firm hand.

"Come on boy, it's time to go."

He took me and led me down the street by my shoulder away from the Green Hag, the butcher's shop and Haight Street. I was mute. I envied the butcher his good fortune to be married to the wildcat Clarice. After the paving stone execution, I hated the butcher. But I better understood the man who kept me from Clarice's bed. Her arms were the only place I found real happiness or would be able to forget a world turned upside down just hours before.

James drove up Buena Vista Avenue West.

"Whoa, stop, stop!" I yelled.

I stood in the passenger seat of the sputtering automobile and hollered, "Aidan! Aidan McCurren!"

A small pale boy stepped out of the shadows at the vine covered side of the street.

"Get in the automobile, boy. I don't know what you're doing here but you're coming back to Sausalito with us now."

Aidan was overjoyed to see James and me. He climbed in between us and offered up his last sausage.

Chapter Twelve

Finney kept his horse on the soft even ground between the pair of tracks. Gravel and ties skirted the lightly grassy path. The track was more than wide enough for the fast horses stolen from the train. They had been riding hard for over an hour. The mayhem and destruction witnessed as they rode the forgotten tracks was wholly unexpected. As though traveling the desert, they found no more trouble like that at the train, but the scenes of devastation were of a similar caliber. They were in the center of a long defile just south of the city, when ahead he spied one of the few overpasses. Finney stopped and waited, his large chestnut mare drank from a clear puddle between a pair of ties. Margie, then deputy Doolen, eventually caught up to him.

"Here's water," he said. The horses snuffled grass and drank noisily.

"You two notice the sky up ahead? You smell the burning?"

They had.

"No way to know what we're riding into. If it's as bad as it smells and what we've ridden past we might want to just bolt into the city as fast and as hard and as circuitously as we can."

Margie agreed.

"I don't give two damns about the bank. We got insurance and we're diversely invested. Most of the capital we own is out of state these days. The houses Lucas and I built on Buena Vista Avenue are standing. I know they are because we built them to stay standing. That's where my heart is and that's where I want to head. I say we cut over now and make for the beach. Run up to the Dutch windmill and back into town through the park, if we can.

"Business can wait," Margie agreed, "I vote west and then in through the park."

Deputy Doolen told them, "My family lives on Clayton Street. I don't need go downtown now, not since Tanner's dead."

"Okay, then we're agreed. Next place we see we can get out of this trench, we take it. I don't like being down below everyone, strategic disadvantage even if we are for the most part able to ride unseen."

As he spoke, a man's head poked out from above the side of the distant overpass.

Deputy Doolen slowly drawled, "What in hell does he want?"

Margie and Finney turned and looked where the deputy stared.

Finney passed the rifle and box of shells to Margie, "Move over to the side under that elderberry tree and keep an eye on us would you dear?"

She took the rifle and tugged the reign gently.

The head on the overpass called down, "Where's the train?"

Finney called back, "Quake blew the train up in San Jose, friend."

After a moment, the man yelled down, "All them was on board dead?"

"Everyone made it off alive. Railroad made arrangements to put them up at a local place until they get the tracks clear."

To the deputy, and Margie under the branches of the elderberry tree, he quietly said, "I say "now" and you shoot him if you can, Margie, and we all ride like hell under and away from here."

"I have him, say the word."

She held the rifle to her shoulder and sighted down the barrel like the crack shot she was.

Deputy Doolen added, "He ain't alone. If they have rifles and a mind to firing, at least one of us will get hit if we leave them standing."

The man above called down, "Was you on the train?"

"No, we weren't on the train, friend. We just saw the people being lead away and heard the explosion. Railroad sent us ahead to check the line for more damage."

The man on the bridge held something in his hands, something they could not discern from below.

He yelled down, "Track crew passed here long time ago. Do you know the way out of San Jose? Why you riding up the tracks? What you got in them bags on that..."

"Now."

Margie shot the man between the eyes.

Ears ringing with the report and reverberation they spurred, circled and charged under the overpass as men stood and started firing down where they had been.

As they rode under, the men ran to the other side of the overpass. Finney, Margie, and the deputy weaved over and across the tracks passing each other while keeping the horses on solid ground. The men fired but their blundering pistols missed. Out of range, the three riders stopped and looked back. The men were getting on horses and debating the fastest way to intersect the three riders on the tracks.

"You got a shot? Take a shot! Take as many as you can, quick darlin' quick!"

She steadied her mount and brought the rifle to her shoulder again.

Crack, crack, crack.

Three men fell from their horses onto the bridge.

Crack, crack, crack.

One more tumbled from his mount and from the bridge with a thump as the last two hurried off toward the west.

"Fandango! Here we go."

Finney rode to the man's broken body. He lay across the tracks, more than dead. Finney spat and rode back to his companions.

Finney and the deputy transferred themselves from their spent mares onto the two fresh animals with the secured bags. Each rider's ears sang like a massive soprano in an opera house. They secured the other bags behind their saddles.

"Here we go, hard as hell."

They rode north looking for an escape to the east.

Finney called, "That was one of the Tanner brothers. I don't know which but I wager the other two are looking to find us now. Suppose they planned to bust their brother off the train? Guess the quake put a stop to that. Shame she missed the last two but what a shot, eh, deputy?"

Margie called, "I hit each one I tried for, from horseback and twenty yards below. The last two spooked. There was nothing I could do about them."

Deputy Doolen agreed, "She's one helluva shot."

Eventually they found a gated stand of worn wooden access stairs rising from the level of the tracks to the town above.

"Here we go," Finney said again.

He jumped from his horse and began battering a brass lock with the handle of the large revolver he pulled from his belt. The lock shattered on the third strike.

Finney mounted the stairs and ran all the way to the top. Again, they heard him hit another lock. He ran back down.

"Getting to old for this," he was breathing heavily. "If we lead them the horses can make it up, but not back down."

He grabbed his chestnut's reigns and led her up the stairs speaking to her soothingly the entire time. Margie and the deputy followed, each calmly leading their horse slowly up the wooden service stairs.

At the top, they stood in a town deserted. Buildings skewed. Streets buckled. They saw the fires from the city more clearly and could more accurately discern the scope of the disaster. Finney slowly climbed into his mare's saddle.

"West. We make west and avoid the last of the Tanner gang too."

Margie and the deputy saddled up.

"Where are we?"

"This was San Miguel City. There's Ocean Avenue. We can ride this all the way west through Rancho Laguna de la Merced to the Great Highway," deputy Doolen observed pointing toward the ocean.

They turned the horses west and rode quickly down the deserted street.

"We used to call this Old Ocean House Road, it hooks into Ocean House Road in a minute or two," Finney told them.

Soon they left the city blocks crammed with broken houses and rode in dark seclusion through the Rancho Laguna de la Merced.

The Rancho was a watershed with two large fresh-water lakes. They partially provided drinking water for residents of San Francisco. The sun faded behind the thicket of trees leaving shadows to encroach. The riders felt chilled on their dark trek through the Rancho. Time slowed, measured by the breathing of the horses. Hooves clopped in hypnotizing rhythm on the dirt path along which they rode.

Each rider occasionally turned their head to check for pursuers. Margie made the mistake of looking into the trees and spied small round pale faces studying their fleet progress. She knew the stories of the Rancho Laguna. Murdered ranchers and betrayed soldiers took shape in her mind along the edges of the path with vengeful boney hands and sudden low branches pulling or knocking riders from their mounts.

She recalled the tails of riders and Sunday strollers dragged through the thickets to the lakes and below the surface into their depths, eaten alive by aquatic demons while slowly drowning. She rode through occasionally in a leisurely carriage or in an automobile when younger. She did not recall the overgrowth looking so menacing or appearing so haunted. Sinister wood sprites and evil ogres filled her thoughts as she tried to focus on the horizon by staring straight ahead.

The pale moon faces of those children and adults hiding in the trees did not make her confident of what they might find in their city. What if everyone had gone mad and San Francisco was now hell on earth? The dark wood of the Rancho made her feel cold to her bones. Spittle flecked from her mount's nostrils and mouth and flicked onto her face. She wiped the stringy spit away with a sleeve that ended in fine English lace at her hand. As the small company made the turn onto the latter half of Ocean Avenue her horse's hard breathing became audible to Finney and deputy Doolen.

They slowed and looked at one another, looked at her glossy wet coat.

"Hop on with me, she's beat."

Margie handed the rifle to Finney, grabbed his belt and pulled herself from her saddle to the rear of his as they slowly trotted. She took the rifle in both hands and kept her arms around his chest. They left the mare in the middle of the Rancho. She refused to consider the fine horse's fate; fodder or friend to whoever claimed her next. Margie's eyes were streaming from the cold air. She shut them, imagined herself with Finney, warm and cozy in their bed on the train with the soothing sound of the rails and the rocking of the cars keeping them still, keeping them wound around one another.

He was so old, she thought. He was old when she was born. He lived life multiple times over before her parents were married. He was one of those old men who never became old in his own mind. He acted like a boy. He said he felt like a boy. He made her feel like a girl.

"He is my Miner Forty-Niner," she thought, "Thank God my parents did not name me Clementine."

They rode hard and found themselves headed north on the Great Highway sooner than anticipated. Fresh horses and lack of strangers kept their progress quick and unchallenged. The clear ocean breeze cut past them and whipped each horse's mane, tail, and Margie's hair wildly. Finney and deputy Doolen rode with a hand on their hats. The breakers crashed on distant rocks and a fine mist of chill salt water sprayed them lightly.

As they approached the west end of the park, they passed the construction of Murphy's windmill. Finney called out, "That Sam Murphy is a God damn dummy. Everyone knows one windmill is enough out here."

"I think it is grand of Sam to help build a second one. It will add balance and symmetry to this corner of the park.

Besides, what if the Dutch windmill breaks? It always pays to have a backup plan, Finney."

They rode past Murphy's unfinished windmill and soon turned the horses into the park. They stopped at the massive Dutch windmill and watered at a convenient trough.

"If we want to take the trails we need to start on them here. They get pretty hilly and I don't know that these track horses can take too much rough terrain without tearing up their legs."

"The park seems pretty peaceful, what if we try the main roads and double back to the horse paths if we run into too much trouble?"

Deputy Doolen agreed with Margie.

They mounted again. Margie and Finney traded with the deputy to give the poor mare a lighter load. Trotting slowly Finney called, "If we can't figure out who these two belong to maybe we can just stable them here in the city once all the mess has been cleaned up. Or take them down to the ranch."

Deputy Doolen said, "someone's gonna miss these horses. I never had a smoother, faster ride in my life."

Margie looked behind her and traced her finger along the brand on the chestnut's haunch.

"Someone will be looking for them. They might be willing to let us buy them when all is said and done."

Deputy Doolen smiled and added, "You're assuming the United State's Marshal Service won't impound them, or at least one of them."

Grinning, Finney said, "You got us beat there deputy. I know you fellows are salaried now but every bit helps, yes? You ever want to quit Marshaling and go private, let me know. We'll get you set you up at a bank or with the

Pinkertons. Or whatever you like."

"I just might take you up on that offer, sir. I just might."

As they rode, they heard distant shots from the north. Smoke from small fires burned in all the far intersections. They smelled the disaster of the city. It mixed with the taint of the Pacific shore and pungent eucalyptus berries on the trees in the park.

Chapter Thirteen

At the waterfall, in the grass near the road, two large men in dark suits held another in a disheveled linen suit down. They had apparently forced him from the road and waylaid him, pulling him from his auto for the beating they now gave freely. The large auto was loaded with wooden cases marked "Veuve Clicquot".

Finney stopped their horse, removed the rifle from Margie's hands and put the stock to his shoulder. Deputy Doolen placed a hand on the rifle and slowly lowered the barrel, "Mister McCurren, vigilante justice has very little time and place. This is my job. My park. I'm an armed deputy U.S. Marshal. If you and the lady wait here, I will rejoin you in a moment."

Without pause, he spurred the mare ahead and ran up on the men. They squatted in mid punch, fists pulled back. Deputy Doolen ran the mare into the closer one knocking him across their victim into the other. In a single motion, he slid from the saddle and landed hard blows on the men in dark suits. They were on their backs after a short scuffle.

Their victim, a large man in the linen suit, was still. Deputy Doolen backed away from them as he kept his revolver pointed at the three men. Finney and Margie rode up as he kicked the man in the linen suit in his ribs, spurring him into consciousness.

"I tell you it was easier when the only penalty a law man faced for shooting the lawless was paying their burial fee. I said it before, I'll say it again: Statehood and all her complications will be the ruin of this great land."

"This here," Deputy Doolen said catching his breath and indicating the no longer unconscious victim with a nod, "is Tommy Washington. Tommy's a known thief and a petty larcenist. These other two are Danny and Manny Tender. The three usually work pretty well together but I guess the brothers finally tired of Tommy's endless anecdotes. That right boys?"

One of the dark suited men mumbled, "He never stops talking."

The other chimed in, "He stopped talking now though, oh boy has he."

"Stand up, boys, and come on over here. Now since you were beating on another outlaw and I think I recovered what ya'll stole and this is a day of too much trouble already, I'm releasing you. All three of you. To your own worst devices. I'll keep the auto to return with this stolen liquor. I won't bother asking where they came from. You would each lie and make me more angry and frustrated."

The three men looked at one another blankly. They looked at their three captors.

"Or my partner, Finney "One Punch" here can shoot you with that rifle. I think at this range, Finney, you might be able to take all three down with one slug. What you think?"

"Hell, if I had my way I'd have started shooting from twenty yards back. Avoid all this talk. I guess back in my day there was less talking because the outlaws had spines. Lawman tried talking to an outlaw, they was liable to pull a knife or a hidden gun, no matter what. If these three here nincompoops are the criminal of today I sure ain't worried." Finney spat on the ground.

"You heard the man. You three sorry morons can stand here and he can shoot you or you can start running and he'll take his best, maybe one of you will make it to the street alive!"

Deputy Doolen shot the ground at their feet and they

jumped and ran. They scrambled past the horses and ran zigzags to the closest break in the trees where they could make for Lincoln Avenue. Finney trailed them with the rifle and fired half-hearted shots close enough to keep them moving.

The three bunglers gone, deputy Doolen asked, “You want to drive home or ride home, ma'am?”

Finney helped her down from the back of his saddle as she replied, “Ride.”

Margie adjusted the stirrups on the deputy's mare and swung herself up into the saddle.

Taking the rifle from Finney and shaking off the shock of the day's events, she spoke to the deputy, “Often when situations of moral or ethical dilemma present themselves Finney tells a story from his past that illustrates the clearest choice to be made under the most dire and desperate of circumstances.” She looked at her husband,

“Finney dear, does any tale, true or tall, come to mind to make clear for deputy Doolen why he should have shot all three of those men while he was in possession of the chance?”

Finney smiled at her and removed a bent cigar from his vest pocket.

“If I wasn't near speechless with consternation over their flight I might be able to procure from thought and memory a time or two when mercy, or laziness, later sunk her sharp teeth into a merciful person's exposed behind. What do you two say we open one of those crates and try their stolen bubbly? It must be getting on near past noon and I know I for one am parched in a way I forgot possible.”

Deputy Doolen smiled, “I have to return these crates to their rightful owner, along with this automobile.”

Margie's nostrils flared.

"Now see, that is exactly what I mean. Lawmen aren't good or bad because they are good people and the villains are bad people. Good lawmen are effective for the same reason good horse trainers are effective or good bankers are effective. It is not because they are high minded and morale. It's because they are wise and creative."

Finney added, "The creative man, woman and child will always be creative but the morale man, woman and child will eventually become immoral. Then you have to watch out. There are no hard and fast rules in life. Each circumstance has its own beginning, middle and end.

"High minded action is great in large situations, life altering situations with ramifications upon many folks. Even then, it's a stretch for most folks. When applied to every trivial daily life encounter regularly, high minded folks often snap and stop applying their high mindedness to the larger situations in life in trade for staying high minded in the trivial."

He paused and scanned the bushes.

"You just let three known criminals go. Now they can come back and kill us. Ambush you and take these goods. Or start attending Mass and donating all their time to the good work of the saints. Regardless, but now you tell the folks who rescued you from death, multiple times, and from trying circumstances, they cannot partake in a swallow or two of recovered stolen bubbly. Why? Because it might be wrong.

"Life offers her own rewards. I have known the leaders of this state for over fifty years. I have bought and sold men. Taken and given when the circumstances were right. According to the circumstances. I now tell you candidly what the Honorable Governor Pardee might tell you himself were he here right now. In fact, I think he gave me these cigars. The correct thing to do when you find a stolen lot of goods and three known thieves on a day when your railroad and most of the towns you grew up in are apparently in flames, is to punish the Wicked and reward the Just. It saves everyone a heap of trouble. Especially God and the Just. Next time shoot them and keep a bottle of bubbly for yourself.

Margie added, "Put another way, Deputy Doolen, women and men and children who see the world in black and white, good and evil, can only be black and white, good and evil. The problem is no one is ever all one or the other in reality. This eventually undermines a good person's confidence and many who start out thinking they are all good eventually become all evil without knowing they ever traded sides.

"Those of us who see the world in gray tones, who know extremes are unhealthy, often do good things and sometimes do bad things but usually the line is so smeared we do what we reason is right and has as few possible damaging repercussions as humanly possible." She sighed, "We need to go Finney. Deputy Doolen needs to return his prize and we need to get home to ours."

She turned her mare and galloped away.

Finney raised his hat, "Been a pleasure son. You ever want a job in the private sector you look me up at the bank. You might make a fine Pinkerton, too."

Finney spurred his horse and took off to catch up with Margie. Around the bend, he found her standing beside her horse. She was picking through a smashed Veuve Clicquot crate.

As Finney rode up she said, "Most of them are smashed but I found three intact, so far."

She fished out six unbroken bottles. Finney placed them as securely as he could in his shallow coat pockets and under various straps on his saddle.

Margie peeled the foil from one and removed the little wire cage. She expertly worked the cork with her fine long thumbs and popped the cork into her hand. A white flow of champagne bubbled from the mouth of the bottle. She leaned over the flow and loudly slurped what she could. The flow stopped and she tipped the bottle for a long slow nose-bubbling draught.

Handing the bottle to Finney she said, "That man made me angry. Naiveté and presumption always frustrate me."

Finney said, "Some fellows never get past the fact that life's questions not only have no right answers but don't actually exist or matter. Hell, the asking of the questions distracts from the answer, which in my opinion is the full and active living of life itself."

He tipped the bottle back for a long, bubbly drink.

Chapter Fourteen

Bobby Watson watched the sky over Buena Vista Park. Dark smoke blew away from Ashbury Heights even as ash accumulated on his shoulders like so many sins returned to be counted. Bobby was funny looking. His skin was oily, his teeth were dark. Little brown holes showed in some of them. His small little chin made him ugly. His pal, Curtis Oliver, was handsome, powerfully built with clear skin, straight teeth and a strong protruding jaw. Women asked Bobby who Curtis was when they walked down busy streets.

The whores at the Green Hag bought them drinks and gave it to them both for free on Curtis's good looks alone. Bobby and Curtis lived with their mother's near the west end of Golden Gate Park on the south side near Lincoln Avenue. They met as boys so many years earlier swimming in the frigid Ocean Beach surf every morning. They still swam together each morning.

"Edgar Pepper is fucking dead, mate."

Bobby Watson raised his eyebrows as he whispered this to Curtis. They stood watch on the front stoop of the McCurren house.

"I seen him drive off with the Duke and the Prince and then I heard shots. I ran up over the hill and hid behind that house what fell with the babe in it,"

"Spencer house."

"The same. I seen the Duke and the Prince get back in their ride. I snuck in for a closer look. I seen Edgar Pepper. I seen them tattoos he had all over is left arm."

"Good. Edgar Pepper was a right bastard and deserved to die. Surprised it took the Duke so long to hand in the deed. Probably wanted to get the Prince in on it. Nothing like that happens without the Lieutenant and the Old Man knowing it was in the works."

"Yeah okay," Bobby Watson whined, "But if it can happen to Edgar fucking Pepper it can happen to me or fucking you, right?"

"No. Edgar was a right bastard and deserved to die. If the family left it for much longer, I might have done it myself. I hated him. He was a right bastard."

"Okay, he was a right bastard, but what keeps it from happening to one of us?"

"You ever go in the houses without any of the principals? You ever skim more cash than you could explain? You ever get drunk and try to make it with the Duke's girlfriend on the Duke's dingy?"

"I never done anything like any of that," Bobby Watson said aghast, "it never even occurred to me to do any of that. I like the principals. I love the Lieutenant and the Duke as they were my own family. They was there when me old man were kilt off the coast of Cuba."

"Exactly. That's the tip of the arrow: that's the point. Edgar Pepper had been the Governor's man. Driver even. He got himself kicked down here by the Governor for the principals to keep an eye on. I heard the old man tell the Lieutenant and the Duke the Governor hated Edgar Pepper. Said the Governor found Edgar Pepper's teeth sucking repugnant."

"Me Ma said the same thing."

"Yer Ma?"

"That morning she met him after he passed out in the driveway at the wheel of his motor and we made him have breaky with us after the swim."

"Yeah."

"She sait he was repugnant and she called him "a

weeping twat."

"I know that to be a lie, Bobby Watson," Curtis Oliver laughed.

"I swear it Curtis," Bobby Watson said holding up two grimy fingers on his right hand. "I swear it on my poor dead Da's pension."

"Then your Ma was right dead on," Curtis Oliver cocked his head, "You hear that?"

"I hear an auto working up the hill."

Bobby Watson cradled a double-barrel shotgun nearly as long as he was tall with the stock in the crook of his right elbow. An automobile did come into view from around the curve. They spotted right away it was the Duke with two young Princes.

James pulled the automobile up to the curb in front of Bobby Watson and Curtis Oliver. He killed the motor and pulled the parking brake as the automobile started to roll a little.

"Two Princes," Bobby Watson whispered to Curtis Oliver.

"Boys, anything going on up here?" James called to the men on the stoop as he lifted Aidan McCurren into his arms and onto his broad shoulders.

"No sir, Mister Pritchard," Curtis Oliver replied.

"We found a would-be house breaker and confessed stowaway at the bottom of the hill."

Aidan smiled and held up a raw red sausage.

"Apparently he's also a hungry sausage thief. Samaritan Fundenburg and his bitch chased him under a house down on Central. Can one of you square it with old Sam when you have time or think about in the next few weeks?"

I said, “I'll take care of it.”

James looked at me, his closest friend's oldest boy.

“Never mind boys,” James said, “Any grub for a little guy to clean up in the kitchen?”

Bobby Watson put the shotgun aside, lifted Aidan from James's shoulders, and placed him firmly on the top stair of the stoop.

He took the sausage from Aidan, “Come little princeling, let's us fry this one up with some t'others. I'm a might bit, tid bit peckish meself.”

Aidan smiled and went with Bobby Watson into his house, hand in hand. He was wide-eyed by the very large gun Bobby Watson carried under his other arm.

“I need to tell you Edgar Pepper is no longer with us. Curtis, I want you to take over his responsibilities and see to the tutelage of young Mister Thomas here. Is that a-okay with you?”

James spoke with his hand on Curtis Oliver's large right shoulder.

“It's right as rain with me, Mister Pritchard. That Edgar Pepper was a right bastard, if you don't mind my speaking so, sir,” Curtis Oliver smiled.

“I don't mind at all.”

He reached into his jacket pocket and pulled out a brick of currency. He handed the brick to Curtis Oliver.

“This is what Edgar Pepper was owed and the extra bit owed to you and Bobby Watson. I deputized Thom here this morning and his father and his grandfather know what the plan is or at least knew before today's tragedy accelerated his time for inclusion. No secrets from Thom, a-okay Curtis?”

“Okay, boss.”

Curtis smiled at us, took James' hand, and shook it like a hungry cat shaking a dead rat. They heard hoof beats and listened.

I said, "The Park."

We stood shoulder to shoulder and watched two riders approach the house squarely from the park. The horses cantered and traveled around slightly as each rider took their turn drinking from their own very large dark bottle.

Curtis said, "Looks a bit like the old man and his new bride."

As they approached, Finney raised an empty champagne bottle in salute to the men gathered around the front stoop of his house. His family's house. For the first time that long day was able to feel his coffee had worn off. He was a bit drunk from the fine French champagne. Margie tipped her bottle back and held her hair in place. As she brought the bottle down, she slowly and deliberately raised herself in the stirrups and belched, loudly. Finney and the men looked at each other, looked at her and laughed. It was the only funny thing to happen that entire sad day.

They stopped their horses at the railing and looked about the street. Bobby Watson opened the front door and emerged with Aidan on his shoulders. Each had a sausage and cheese sandwich in his hand and munched heartily with bulging cheeks. Aidan smiled at his grandfather and gaped at the fine, bristling beige mare beneath him.

"Where'd you get that horse, Finney? You ride all the way back from Los Angeles?"

Finney smiled at the moon-eyed boy.

"Nope. We rode up from San Jose. Stole these horses and their tack off the train right before she blowed up."

Aidan smiled, "I stole sausages from the butcher. I

thought he was gonna blow up!"

Margie opened another bottle of champagne, took a long bubbly swig that burned her small nose and handed the bottle down to go around. As each man took a long draught, Finney studied the front of the house, asked after everybody and word of the damage.

"We seen the fires. Seems you can't sink a barge in the bay without everything downtown catching fire. Where's Laurence? Where are the kids?"

"I saw him a bit ago, Gramps. He and his men are down at Market and Van Ness. He's okay. Should be here shortly. Everyone else is fine, James sent them to Sausalito."

Finney sighed.

"Any fresh coffee? We ain't had any since about four this morning and that bottle is pulling me down."

Bobby Watson told us, "There's fresh and strong boiling right now. Just made enough for everyone. We'll bring it on out, right Princeling?"

Aidan ducked and they went back into the house, sandwiches eaten.

"Was your train moving when the big quakes hit, Margie?" James asked.

She and Finney looked like desperadoes. They wore cartridge belts and little chunks of earth and mud-splatter clung all over them. Two small black grips and a lock box lashed to their saddles. The horses were foaming and each rider had at least two pistols at the ready. Margie balanced a rifle in her reigns' arm and held the returned bottle of bubbling wine in her other hand.

"Oh my God. I had not thought of that, James. No. Thankfully, we were at San Jose station for the largest quakes. If we were moving, we would probably be dead. The tracks we rode past on our way here looked like vengeful circus elephants pulled them aground. We were sitting on the tracks when the largest hit. It crumbled the station and tipped the water tower before our eyes. It wet us from outside the car, lifted part of the train, with our car, off the tracks, and put us back down again off the tracks.

The men gaped. Margie continued.

"Finney got us out safely. We stole five horses from a livestock car and made it a safe distance before the entire depot and train exploded in a cloud of gas."

"Everything's gone except what we have here," Finney added.

"So much death today. I suppose it is not over."

James asked, "You see Bob Tanner?"

"I surely did," Finney grinned. "Saved the deputy guarding him too. I killed three on that train including Tanner. Margie shot four more in an ambush up the line. We know for sure one of them was a Tanner brother. Another two we missed. Luckily, they never turned up again. Suppose they'll show up here or down at the bank eventually. Any word on the bank?"

"I sent men on down this morning. Pinkertons is out of men. I never heard back from the first group so I secured more men from the Green Hag an hour ago to go down after they form up here before sunset."

The door opened and Aidan and Bobby Watson returned with trays of toasted cheese bread, fried sausages and steaming cups of hot coffee. I secured the two tired horses as Finney and Margie and the elders gripped coffee and chewed sausages held by cheesy toast. I removed the remaining bottles, weapons, box and bags from the saddles.

I removed each horse's tack, sent Aidan for two

brushes, and filled the front trough with water from the pump.

James held the rifle taken from the train employee and asked Margie, "You shoot the four Tanner's with this piece?"

"Yes I did. Down on the tracks up at an overpass, about thirty yards. My ears are still ringing."

They heard shots in the distance and stopped chewing.

Curtis Oliver informed them, "Mayor declared marshal law this mornin'. Declared looters shot on sight. Nation Guard is patrolling with their regular troops. The damage is everywhere but the fire is mostly downtown. Almost every park's turned into a camp for refugees and fire victims."

Finney asked, "What's our plan?"

"Our families are staying at Abigail's family estate in Sausalito. They will remain where they are until the fires and the peace are resolved. We secured and paid enough barges, teamsters and men to start demolition the minute the brigades extinguish the fires. Or sooner. The properties we own are as secure as we can make them and all of our people and their families are as safe and comfortable as we can make them.

"I have Donald going over all of Ashbury Heights and the damage reports as we get them. He's as good an engineer and builder as any and better than most. He says we'll be ready to start building before any other neighborhood in the city. I believe him."

Donald Pritchard was James and Abigail's son. A city engineer, he built three buildings in Ashbury Heights in the previous five years. After the quake, they were all still standing.

"We'll need additional ready funds from the vault downtown in two days but I figure as long as we keep track of expenditures the Federal boys should pay us back at least ninety to ninety five cents per dollar we spend on reconstruction. Maybe more."

Finney asked, "Any word on the governor? Was he in town?"

"My understanding from the boys at the Green Hag is he was in Sacramento and doing fine. It didn't hit Sacramento too badly. We need to get going if we're to be across the bay before sunset. I still have some stops to make and travel across town, as you can imagine, by auto or wagon is slow." James looked at the face of his gold pocket watch.

"You two can come with us or ride to the pier if you want to stay across the bay. You know you're welcome and everyone would be glad to see you. You would have to ride armed, I don't know if that's too tiring after the ride you made today."

Margie said, "I am spent. I have no desire to stay in a house that needs to be protected by armed guards."

"No," Finney said. "We'll come with you boys, just need to secure these things and take a private moment upstairs myself. My backside ain't used to riding like we did today."

Finney grabbed the bags and was inside and up the stairs in a flash.

Margie spoke to one in particular, "He stabbed three men today. I shot mine from far away. Oh, and I closed a man's head in a livestock door then kicked him in his face.

She sighed and fingered the thick champagne bottle.

"Finney saved a deputy U.S. Marshal's life a few times

today. He killed that Bob Tanner when he held Deputy Doolen at a disadvantage, after the initial quake. We brought him off the train with us before the explosion. We took down the men who waited to ambush and remove Mr. Tanner from the train."

She looked up and studied the strange horrific sky.

"We rode into the park, and after all this blood, after the hard ride and switching horses and all the destruction we witnessed along the way, the deputy decided to return a load of recovered champagne to whomever it was stolen from. We were a bit surprised when his morality jumped ahead of the events and the situation of the day. Realistic morality versus moral realism. Faced with continued unknowns and actions we took today, his mind opted for the easiest of tasks he found at hand. Returning stolen goods to their rightful owner."

James said, "I paid lying, drunken degenerates large amounts of money to keep them from preying upon the innocent I represent. To help us rebuild the community of the innocent. I have no qualms with my means justifying my ends. We shot men today. Thom and I witnessed a beheading on Haight Street. Children and old people lie broken and dying on sidewalks under piles of rubble. God's temples, churches and hospitals are burning and obliterated. So a deputy U.S. Marshal returns stolen liquor. We've known deputy Marshals our entire lives. They deputized Laurence and me when we were the age. Lucas and Finney were deputies too. I don't think I've ever heard of a Marshall returning stolen goods. Shooting bad guys, escorting prisoners, saving the innocent were the kind of Marshaling we practiced."

"I'm thinkin'," Curtis Oliver said, "realistic morality

and moral realism, philosophy and premeditation go out the window and into the bay when your city is burning and you're confronted with immediate and continually possible kill situations. There's no philosophy necessary for instinct and training, all action is truth. You either fall back on what you know to do and quiet your mind into a calculated procession of sustaining actions or you get shot and die."

"Precisely', Margie agreed, "The philosophy of instinct is also the doctrine of survival. I suppose my qualm with deputy Doolen was his sudden lapse into thought and subsequent panic disguised as impervious moral rectitude."

Finney returned from the house and stood on the front porch.

"Problem with Deputy U.S. Marshal Doolen is he never killed a man and found himself afraid he may have to this day. Problem is it makes him and any man or woman depending on him as good as dead on a day of misery like today. He kept me from killing those men and then he avoided killing them too. They looked like they already killed today. I bet you a shiny silver dollar they doubled-back and took him out of that auto the minute he rolled onto Lincoln Avenue. Day like today is Christmas to a bad man. Kill anyone you want to kill, rape anyone you want to rape, rob anyone you want to rob. Without enough law to go around there's little chance of justice or retribution at the hand of woman or man."

Finney tossed a box of shells to Margie.

"See if these are right for that gun, darling."

He handed more rifles out of the house to the other hired men gathered to protect the interests of the citizens at the top of Loma Vista.

"I'm roasting up more coffee berries to take across to

Sausalito, just five more minutes and I'll be ready to go," Finney went back into the house.

They heard a wagon approaching from the east and waited with guns ready in the crooks of their elbows. Three blackened firefighters sat on the bench of smart little cabriolet. Two big red wheels crunched over bricks and mortar, a big horse lunged to get the men over the troughs and valleys of disheveled paving stones. From far away the men appeared obviously spent.

They slouched and swayed with every step the large black horse took. The men rocked together, should to shoulder. The cart came to rest before the group gathered at the front of the McCurren home. Aidan squealed with the recognition of his father and ran down the steps to the end of the walk. Laurence McCurren smiled and took his young son up in his arms as he stepped out. Soot and filth blackened each man.

The men shivered and stamped with cold as their damp legs and arms absorbed the west wind that blew across the top of the hill and park. Hugging his father blackened Aidan.

As his father rested him on the ground, Aidan asked, "Are you hungry father? Want a hot cup of coffee? Grandpa Finney is roasting and popping coffee berries in the kitchen, I'll ask him to fry more sausages and make you and your men some toasted cheese."

Aidan took the steps two at a time and ran into the house yelling for Finney at the top of his lungs. Margie and the men around the front of the house stared at the brigade men, speechless.

Standing before a handful of lucky surviving San Franciscans, they looked like the fire and destruction left behind downtown.

"Thom, go get a bottle of your father's best whiskey from the built-in in the front dining room," Margie said.

As I ran up the steps, she walked forward, gave Laurence a tight hug around his filthy neck, and placed a tear-stained kiss on a cheek covered with soot.

She backed away from him wiping tears from her face.

"We were so worried about you and our family. What a relief to find everyone safe and whole," she sniffed slightly. "Introduce us to these young men."

Laurence introduced his sergeants and Margie shook their hands, gave them a tearful peck on the cheek and introduced the family's security men and the Pinkertons.

I returned with a new bottle. Margie peeled the tax paper and removed the large cork with her teeth. She handed the bottle to one of the young sergeants. He looked at Lieutenant McCurren. The Lieutenant nodded and the young man took a sip. The fine aged single-barrel liquor tore his throat and made his red-rimmed eyes water and raw nose begin to run.

He handed the bottle to his Lieutenant who tipped it up and took a long slow drink. The bottle passed from the firefighters to the security men to Margie and me. Finney took the bottle when he returned with another tray of food and coffee. The firefighters fell upon the food and coffee as Finney took a long swallow from a bottle now almost empty.

After a second sandwich and a cup of strong hot coffee Laurence said, "We left it burning but contained. The damage is nearly total from Van Ness to the bay. It won't spread any further west if we can continue the hard work. We took this buggy from Auxiliary Bishop Augustus. He'll expect it back before long but I wanted to get a bit of rest and to feed the two young men here."

He turned to his young sergeants.

"Take what you think the lads might need. Thom will show you where the linens and the supplies are. Pick the Auxiliary Bishop up in his buggy, and then have him drop you and your supplies off at the fire line. This is very important. If the Auxiliary Bishop feels you neglected him or you did not return as quickly as you could he'll be very displeased and I don't need him displeased with us today. Thom, give them at least one more bottle of this whiskey to take to Auxiliary Bishop Augustus. You met him earlier and saw him under dire circumstances. Anything else you can think of he might require down there, give it to these lads to take to him, okay?"

Aidan brought oats for the large black horse while I showed the two firefighters to the kitchen and the pantry. I ran to the third floor and began hefting sheets and towels from the missing wall into the waiting cabriolet below.

"No problems on the honeymoon Finney?"

"Nope," Finney grinned. "Just this damn quake and what looks from here like the fires of hell trying to engulf our city. Any word on the bank?"

"None. Assume the worst."

"You lose many men today son?"

Finney looked at Laurence. Laurence's eyebrows knitted and he looked at his hands.

"We had a collapse and can't account for ten of the men from the Ashbury Heights ladder crew. They were manning two hoses and got too close to see what was happening. We hollered and I had runners positioning other crews but they left their perimeter mark. We watched it happen. Everyone hollered, they looked at us, they looked up, they looked for their marks and as they realized their folly and ran the building literally jumped and caught them. They're gone. Just gone."

"Did they tell you about the Spencers?" Laurence asked his father.

"We seen their house was gone but I was too afraid to ask. The baby too?"

Laurence nodded.

"Well, they were fine folks. That baby was a cutie. We knew all of them since they were born, eh? Hell, I watched Donald grow up on this street. Buried Donald's mom and dad. We administered the estate until Donald was of age. He was a good friend. Good attorney too. It's a damn shame."

Finney turned with tears on his cheeks and climbed back into the house. Margie walked over to the sight were the Spencer home stood before, now a pile of jagged rubble and smoldering debris.

The wind shifted and sun filtered down through the sky bathing Castro Valley and Noe Valley in light to the south as she surveyed the demolished house. Soft baby clothes, towels, and lacy pillows entwined splintered timbers and mounds of lath, hanging sheets of plaster. A large gray rat scurried along a far timber. Margie walked back to the front of the McCurren house.

She took up the rifle stolen from the man on the train and chambered a round. She shouldered the cherry stock and fired at the curious rodent. It disappeared in the crack of the rifle. She ejected the shell, chambered another round and scanned the pile for more rats. Finney ran from the house pistol drawn but stopped on the stoop when he saw there was no trouble.

"I think the most unexpected part of the quake and fire is the rats," Laurence said. "I grew up with rats, we all did. In the service, there were times when we shipped out and rations were so tight that we were glad to catch a few and roast them. In South America, during the fighting, we saw some as large as small cats. They were bold as brass and began gnawing men as quickly as they fell. I never saw as many as I have seen this morning. Entire boulevards of them come running from collapsing buildings. They run into the sewers and down the streets. Who knows where they might end up? One large building collapsed and as the dust settled and the fires sprang up and the rats ran past us, I swear there were three as large as small ponies."

"That ain't true," James said smiling.

"It is true," Laurence said. His voice was grave. "Sergeant Manus there shot each one of them. Then we washed them into a smoldering blaze."

"I shot each one in the head," Sergeant Manus agreed with his lieutenant.

"One was so large," Laurence continued, "It actually wore a livery bridle. After the sergeant shot the thing, I looked closer and realized there was a brass plate embedded in the bridle's leather. It read, "Algonquin – If Found Please Return to Ted Roosevelt."

Margie stared at Laurence. Each man looked at another and then Finney smiled and began cackling. Margie punched Laurence on the arm and they all laughed.

Laurence smiled and Finney said, "You God damn son of a bitch, I thought you were serious. Hand up that bottle. It's time for us to get a move on. No more talk about rats, and no more pot shots Margie. I'm not loading shot and casting slugs for any man or woman today, no matter how dead-on a shot she is."

I helped the two sergeants secure their supplies in the buggy. As they mounted and slowly turned about Laurence called, "Give me four hours boys."

They waved, nodded, and proceeded slowly down the hill in the direction they had come.

Each McCurren checked their weapons. Aidan sat in the long wagon with his grandfather Finney while James and I sat up front and coaxed the horses. Before we pulled away from the houses on Buena Vista Avenue Finney was snoring lightly. Aidan sat on his lap and watched as Finney's eyes drooped and his head nodded. Margie rode her stolen mare, freshly combed and fed. James Mann, a Pinkerton and professional guard employed by James Pritchard for over seven years rode the other stolen horse, fresh and once again frisky. We rolled down the hill as Laurence walked up the front stoop of his house.

He climbed the front stairs and entered the disheveled bedroom shared with his wife Angela. He removed his charred and ruined uniform and big boots. Naked, he used a sink full of bucket water, Lilly soap and a cotton cloth to wash away the fire. Finished, he wrapped a thick white Turkish robe around himself and fell immediately asleep on the large bed that filled one end of their bedroom. Years of being a fire fighter and living with small children gave him the ability to fall deeply asleep the instant he closed his eyes. He always woke with no idea of the time passed. The sleep of three minutes in a chair in the sitting room before supper seemed the same to him as a full, uninterrupted night.

Their children, like most small children, seemed to believe sleep came faster and better when shared in a group.

Especially in a large warm soft valley of a bed where a loving, bedraggled parent at either far side did their best to feign sleep, elbowed and jabbed by the restless, warmed to sweating by the immobile, struggling to bring it and keep it a while.

Chapter Fourteen

Angela McCurren and Abigail Pritchard directed the house and grounds staff through their exhaustive search of the cellar, attic and shore for Aidan McCurren's anticipated limp and lifeless little body. Each woman was drunk to the point of crying while still sober enough to direct others to precarious outcroppings of rocks. To peer under piers for a body in the wash. To have the cisterns thoroughly prodded.

They inventoried each pantry and every bedroom with housemaids and stable boys. They found a long-missing diamond and sapphire bracelet. A stash of multiple whiskey bottles, nearly one in every room. Cheap photographs of very large and very naked women. Countless broken bits from toys, colorful rocks, and an ocean of seashells. They did not find Aidan McCurren.

Sean McCurren woke from his nap earlier that evening, sleepily found his Ma and Auntie Abigail watching the smoke and boats on the bay from the house's large back sleeping porch. Immediately bored by their unceasing talk of a shared splendid childhood he asked his Ma where Aidan was. She told him he was still asleep in his room, next door to Sean. Sean insisted he was not. Although his mother dismissed him, he finally convinced them to look. The two mothers filled their highballs and followed Sean to Aidan's empty room. Their panic did not start in earnest until a quick questioning of the house and kitchen staff yielded no sight of the boy in three or four quiet hours. After the thickheaded nursemaids were made to cry, an honest search was on.

"I will be damned if my children are to survive the worst disaster to befall or city in forty years only to be washed to sea or smashed to bits in a ravine on the safest land around the bay. He must have snuck back to the city. There are too many people working here today for a precocious child with a flair for devilment to spend an entirely innocent day undisciplined and unadmonished by a single worthy adult."

Angela held her friend's hand as they stood at the end of the small pier where the boat left for the city many hours earlier. She did not cry. She clutched baby Abigail to her chest and scanned the water for any sign of imagined pale ribbons of flesh revealing themselves as swells washed lose clothes across a bloated, drowned, and sunk boy's puckered skin.

"I can send Old Tim across in a skiff, although it is a bit rough looking and God knows there's not enough light left for him to make it confidently across."

Abigail squeezed her friend's small cold hand. The wind from the bay stung their eyes with salt and ash. They smelled the city burning and each fought back a fresh flood of tired tears.

"What chance is there it will rain tonight or tomorrow?" Abigail asked. "Yesterday was so hot. Hot like today. It will be hard to forget the sounds from this dreadful morning on hot mornings to come. Charles told me two more hot days and the rains should pull in from the ocean."

Abigail laughed.

"We shall see. My brother is superstitious about weather, wealth and women."

Angela laughed and covered her mouth with slender fingers.

"He is always dreadfully wrong about each."

"He told me Chief Sullivan and his wife was found dead this morning. Killed in the quake, early, before the fires started. Did you know them? I do not recall ever meeting either of them."

Abigail scanned the bay for a familiar craft.

"No you wouldn't. They were not society. She was very nice. Young and quiet, shy but kind. Her hair was stunning, chestnut colored. Her figure was slight, petite. I met her a few times at official dinners. He was brilliant. They all said so. Laurence especially. But young. If their chief is dead, it is no wonder this blaze has got away from them. I cannot believe they too are dead. And he not from fire but from the quake. They all talk of dying by the blaze. No one wants to be killed, but if they have to die, they say, there would be no better or honorable way to go than like the skipper of a majestic vessel sinking with his ship."

Tears trailed along her delicate cheeks to her fine chin.

"I say they are a bunch of damned fools who need to ask the skipper's grieving widow and fatherless brats how they might prefer their damn patriarch to die. I am thinking Missus Sullivan, at least, died the way she might have preferred. At home. With him. With the man she so obviously cherished and adored. Perhaps it was the true way he preferred too. I hate the Goddamn fire service and its tradition of pensioned widows and mewling orphans. Not the constituency I would actively choose for myself or my babes."

"No man with a family should actively place himself in harm's way," Abigail agreed. "If a man is a father to babies, new or grown, and he has a woman he adores and who adores him, what more could possibly be needed for a full life? I think they consider only themselves, these bastards who fight fires and bank robbers and their stupid wars and climb mountains or trek across the frozen poles leaving grieving and haunted families behind never knowing if the man and father they all love and depend upon is dead or alive."

Small tears ran down Abigail's cheeks too.

"Not knowing if they are dead or alive breaks a heart. If he turns up dead, it breaks a heart. If he is alive, your heart swells but then breaks all the harder when they inevitably spend very little time with those who do love them so. Apparently, they either run off on another foolish endeavor, there will always be more jungles to explore, fires to fight, and robbers to apprehend. Or they publish a memoir so they may tour and lecture, flaunting their self-proclaimed heroics in the envious face of each man sensible enough to stay home with his loving family."

She wiped the tear from her cheek.

"What if we did it? What if we bought a ship and filled it with a crew of gorgeous young sailors? We could go explore the seven seas, find out if climax aboard ship is different with multiple men in varying hemispheres. Native and non-native."

Angela gasped and giggled.

"We could publish our findings in a memoir and tour the country demonstrating the best techniques to women abandoned by adventure-seeking husbands. We could bring our young sailors with us and rent out their services. Adventure In The Boudoir For The Abandoned Wives. The heart-worn women could cease wringing their hands and standing at the post box all day. They would be found on their backs kicking their heels up in primal ecstasy when the news their man was finally located frozen-stiff or starved to death on an island, his corpse hand wholly ignored when finally reached around the globe to gingerly slice the heart out of their widow's bodice."

Angela wept and laughed, "Shut it. Just shut it."

Abigail drained her glass, "A-okay, I shall shut it. Not only because I made myself unspeakably frisky thinking of rocking ships and sweaty young sailors but because I have no more cocktail and now I see our family returning to us, right there."

She pointed to a small white and green sail a few hundred yards to the west.

"Appears as though they were forced to tack a bit," she observed.

As they watched, the crystal salon glass slipped from Abigail's hand and plunked into the shallow water next to the pier.

"Damn," she said under her breath, "Oh well, was empty."

She turned to a stout young spotty house girl who stood twenty feet away and spoke to her in Irish, "Nell, run and tell Cook they are approaching. And tell Old Tim if he gives me another empty glass I shall have to have words with him."

Abigail smiled. The girl blushed and stared.

"Ma'am?"

"I mean," Abigail clarified, "I would like him to mix up another pitcher of cocktails. Just like the last. Tell him they were perfect. Also please ask him to ready a few Toddies." She added with emphasis, "Please."

"Yes ma'am," Nell stammered.

She ran up to the house and inside as quickly as she could.

Abigail addressed the bay, "I don't understand why the help thinks I'm even more of a bore when I'm drunk. I find myself very amusing. Even when I am not drunk, I find myself very entertaining. Perhaps it is they who are the bores and I am a rose amongst the crocus?"

"You said you were going to shut it. I like crocus. It is very difficult to be sad and grieve and watch one's city burn while drunk when you never cease your endless prattle. The new girl hates you drunk or sober because you are her employer. If you worked for you, you would hate you too. It is not personal. It is professional. After she knows you a few years, if she stays that long, she will adore you just like all the rest of us do. Despite our better judgment."

Handing her the sleeping baby, "Hold your namesake; I want to spy at the approaching craft with Charles' glass."

Abigail pressed the warm drooling bundle to her chest as Angela held a small tarnished and dented brass tube to her eye.

Turning one end she said, "I see Margie and Finney. I see Thom and that dratted Aidan and James and some of the lads."

Lowering the glass, "How did he get back to the city? Why? I hate this. If I scold him, it will break my heart further. If I kiss him and hold him the way I want he will only be encouraged to do whatever he likes without fail."

"Darling, he will do whatever he likes without fail no matter what you say or do. Just hold him and tell him how worried you were and maybe he'll leave a note next time or at least be as careful as he must have been this time to be returning to us in one piece."

Baby Abigail cooed and they both looked at her adorable red face as she stretched and yawned.

"I hoped Laurence might be with them. At least that dreadful Father Augustus is not. If he were it would mean something dreadful happened to Laurence."

"I don't mind Father Augustus," Abigail chirped.

"You don't mind Father Augustus because he believes fondling your frighteningly ample bosom is a sacrament."

"I wish he would make it more like communion. He is one very experienced priest. An Auxiliary Bishop now. God definitely tries to keep some of the best for himself."

"I thought you were shutting it."

"I can't help it if you're the only woman in California who hasn't copulated with a priest," Abigail teased.

"Hand me the baby so I can shove you off the pier, you need to retrieve your glass. Priests do not lay with women; it would break their oath to God."

"I did not lay with him; we did it standing up, in a confessional. They are men sweetie, they took an oath but no oath can supersede the biological oath a man has to his privates. You know they cannot go longer than a few days, God forbid a lifetime, without sexual relations. Even Pope Pius has to have an occasional release. Thank God we live in the west. I hear back east they do not prefer girls."

Abigail clutched the sleeping baby tighter as Angela tried to wrest her from her giggling auntie's grip.

Nell returned with shawls for the women and heavy rugs for the chilled sailors. Old Tim followed with a tray of short glasses and steaming tumblers. Charles approached the landing from one of the guest cottages and joined his sister and Angela. He was tall and handsome. He and his sister both favored their mother, now deceased.

His skin was dark, hair black and wavy. He wore expensive hand stitched suits and even more expensive alligator boots. He was a dandy and well known around the bay's horse tracks, sleazier saloons and whorehouses.

"Is our young fugitive among them?" He asked taking a glass from Old Tim's silver tray.

"He is. Finney and Margie are aboard too."

"The smoke looks thicker," Charles observed. "If the heat persists it must rain by the week's end."

Angela and Abigail smiled.

Angela said, "I do hope so, sooner better than later."

"Sooner better than later," Abigail echoed softly.

Chapter Fifteen

"Ahoy!" The call from the yacht.

"Ahoy!" The women called in reply.

As the little craft approached the pier Aidan yelled, "Mama! Mama! Did you miss me?"

He sat on my shoulders, we each grinned with a loving face.

The boat bumped, Aidan and I leaped to the pier. We fastened the ropes securing the vessel and gave mother hugs. She held us, and then looked at Aidan.

"You ever run off like that again and it will be the last time you ever run off like that again, understand young man?" Aidan looked at the ground and said he understood.

We shook hands with Charles and Abigail.

"Run inside and get cleaned up for supper," mother told us. "Thom McCurren, if that's a pistol I felt in your coat pocket you leave it on Tim's tray. You won't need it here."

I fished the heavy revolver from my jacket and placed it on the silver platter with a clatter before a wide-eyed Aidan. As we ran to the house, Charles picked the weapon up and opened the chamber.

Emptying fat bullets into his hand he said, "This gun was fired today. Needs to be cleaned."

Finney and Margie gave hugs and shook hands and Finney said, "We have a bunch more need to be cleaned too. Can we set young Thom up in your study after supper with rags and oil?"

"We can. I might be able to find a few more to benefit from a young man's touch with rag and brush."

"James tells me Thom was field deputized a Marshal this morning. Boy needs to be familiar with the entire process if he's to be kept from turning into a right pain in the ass."

"Is gun cleaning how you kept Laurence from becoming a pain in the ass?" Charles asked with a grin.

"Hell there was no amount of anything his mama or I could do to prevent that from happening. This girl here is what turned him from delinquent to a fellow a man likes to be around."

Finney smiled with pride and held Angela by her small waist.

"Where did he get a badge to give Thom in the field?" She dreaded the answer.

"Edgar Pepper give him his," was Finney's evasive reply.

James heard their exchange and stopped handing the bags off the small yacht. Taking a toddy and thanking Old Tim in Irish he said, "Pepper had plans to take liberties today. He knew I would be carrying large amounts of bills necessary to facilitate peace and immediate reconstruction. Thom was riding with me, you knew that when you left him with me this morning. I didn't keep him for his company, although he is a great, smart young man. I kept him to help me help us. And the neighborhood. And he did."

"Where is Edgar Pepper?" Angela asked.

"I shot him in the debris of the Spencer house and burned his body," a candid confession was expected and given.

Nell walked from the house and told them Cook said supper was on the table.

"Thank you Nell, we'll be right up. Tim, see if cook needs anything from you please."

Finney said, "Edgar Pepper was a rat when he worked for the Governor. One of the reasons he sent Pepper to us. Bigler knew he would either be straightened up or straightened out."

As they walked to the house James told Finney and Angela, "I also showed Thom the safe in your house. You should have seen his face. He told me the linen closet was always off limits. He was pretty surprised."

"We're the only ones with keys and it's kept locked. They know linens go in there but for the most part they don't care about laundry or clean sheets."

"Charles," James called, "Where are you hiding Donald?"

"Oh, I'll send Nell to fetch him; he's holed up in one of the guest cottages pouring over drawings and schematics and plans for new buildings. Been at it all day. Ran across the bay a couple of times to check details on things but for the most part has been in a world of calculation."

"Good, good. My plan now is to start demolition tomorrow, with first light. We have the barges, we have shoreline designated for debris, we have the teamsters, and we have the men. The amount of idle labor will be huge; so many folks now have no jobs. We can keep them busy and productive and in funds."

"You remind me, I need to make a few telephone calls. Are the wires still up here? Are they working to other parts of the state?" Finney asked.

"We'll find out right after we eat," Charles replied.

Uncle Donald Pritchard was wild when he was a child. Quick witted and funny he was the favorite of his grandfather, Lucas Pritchard.

The two were inseparable until Lucas's death a few years earlier. Together they rode horses across the peninsula and the surrounding hills. They sailed the bay and explored the inlets and islands. Donald loved hearing Lucas and

Finney's stories of the rough days in the rough state. Lucas was always his most comfortable on the water or on a horse and he passed his penchant for both to his grandson. Unlike the commonly idle third generations of wealth, Donald was not spoiled, slovenly or lazy. He whistled through his teeth, like Lucas, and he ate with an appetite, like Lucas.

Finney and Lucas taught young Donald how to build. How to appreciate wood, steel, and concrete and how to bring them together to make strong houses and buildings. Donald loved numbers and earned an engineering degree while he attended school in the east. When he returned to San Francisco the family immediately funded buildings of his design.

He quickly became known as a master builder and, to his credit, none of the buildings he designed or constructed fell in the quake. He spent that day feverishly checking the damage of each building, compiling a list of concerns for his crews. He told each owner he would absorb the cost of repairs where applicable. He was coordinating the crews of men and women needed for his father and their anticipated needs to rebuild Ashbury Heights.

Donald's young bride, Melinda, checked his calculations and advised on all aspects of design including structural ideas and sounding-out vague practices. She encouraged him to steer away from brick and block work, to focus on over-poured, reinforced concrete. Their intense marital arguments concerned aggregates, sand quality, and where to buy steel work.

The Pritchards and McCurrens adored Melinda. She got along well with her mother-in-law because they both came from older, wealthier San Francisco families. In addition to assisting Donald on his building projects, Melinda was an active advocate in many of Abigail's favorite charities. Abigail and Melinda's mutual enthusiasm for Mister de Young's Memorial Museum was the catalyst for her introduction to the Pritchard family.

In the early days, when Donald was a small boy and Abigail was a bored mother and wife, the museum was more like a city-subsidized private club. To a woman of idle time, Mister de Young's Memorial Museum was a dream. The finer women of the city spent entire days admiring their husband's treasured donations. Their maiden names were on some pieces, their married names on others, for the entire city to see on the walls below artist's names and in display cases. Their babies happily played together in Golden Gate Park with their nurses. Picnics were eaten and guest lecturers, from around the globe, were wined and dined and entertained when not lecturing.

Abigail's daddy helped found Mister de Young's Memorial Museum to have a secure and relatively inexpensive place to annex his collection of art and rare objects. The founder's insurance companies came up with the idea of a new building with state-of-the-art security and a private staff for maintenance. This lowered their overhead and offset the insurance risk. By charging the general public access to see the precious and rare objects in a secure building, the insurance company had less to lose. Her father and the founding “Old Men” reveled in the idea of payment for owning and collecting what they all considered essential pieces in a full life.

There was never any question of selling a piece or buying less due to the cost of storage or maintenance or insurance. They found the city willing to maintain and manage their collections in a financially beneficial manner for all concerned. All they did was allow the rest of the world access to their treasures in buildings eventually named for their families. The finest and rarest of the collections remained at family homes, the necessary cast offs to make a collection complete, a master's lead-up work and practice work, was hung on the museum's walls or enclosed in public display cases.

The museum was a very large and public vault. The tax credit went to the collectors while the insurance, maintenance and collection costs went to the city. Mister de Young's idea was amazing. At first, the museum kept short and irregular hours for public access and the admission was relatively expensive. A guard stood in each gallery and no children or people of low or foreign birth gained admittance. The original museum board of directors believed no one from Chinatown or Little Italy wanted to see art or pay for the privilege of viewing master works. The board hired directors, curators, kitchen staff and a private security staff and billed the city twice what the board paid.

The museum, founded for the people of the city, profited the wealthy. It eventually evolved into another playground for the wives of the largest collectors and major donors. Their husbands showed themselves on occasional hurried evenings for short private strolls through the halls with a curator following a few paces behind. The collections were theirs and they knew more about the art of the world than anyone they could hire. They knew what to hang and what to hide. They knew what should be extolled because it was brilliant and original. They corrected the misspelled names of the artists and corrected the dates painted. Their wives did this too.

The people of San Francisco eventually recognized the city's elite restricted access to a huge private retreat in one of the world's finest urban parks. They eventually recognized the enormous maintenance and daily expenses paid by the city. The original building even housed a private theater where European and American tours performed the classics and popular shows of the day to exclusive audiences. Lavish furnishings filled the building to accommodate large parties. The main gallery served as a ballroom. One smaller gallery conveniently located near the very large kitchen sat seventy at a massive beautiful cherry table.

Jealous anger from the excluded families and the election of a different-minded mayor forced the de Young into operation as a legitimate museum supported and loved by the people of San Francisco, but Abigail never forgot the heady private days in the beginning.

Chapter Sixteen

"I spoke to the curator of the museum," she Abigail Finney and Margie, "He said they would love the addition of the cameos, the brooches, to the permanent collection."

Margie smiled and squeezed her arm, "So we can keep collecting and they clean, catalog and display them?"

"Yes. Essentially, they house your collection. Every piece you buy and donate is recorded and cataloged as an individual item but added to the collection as part of the whole of the jewelry you already donated."

"Margie, that is wonderful. I picked up a few more down south from a dealer I know. We nearly lost so many on the train. Finney saved them. I decided right then I wanted them in a central and safer place where everyone could see them. Including us. I am tired of fingering them at home in front of the safe. Like a sneak-thief."

"Then it's decided. When all this dies down and they know once again what is going on at the museum I will renew contact and let him know you agree. What do you think Finney?"

Abigail held his arm.

"Hell, I never wore them, I just bought them. Who knew they would become valuable and rare enough to be in a museum. I had no idea I bought enough to call it a collection. You know, four wives might be called a collection by some."

He smiled a tired and whiskery grin as Margie playfully elbowed his skinny ribs.

In Irish Finney asked, "Tim, where's the whiskey, man? I have no stomach for this woman's cocktails or hot gin and honey drinks."

Taking the bottle offered, Finney poured three fingers in two large crystal glasses. Handing one to Old Tim he told the old man, "We're too old to not drink together."

They smiled and drank together.

"I heard you Finney McCurren," Abigail walked over to the two old men.

She took the glass from Finney, smiled and in slurred Irish said, "Pour the old bastard another one, this one's mine."

They sat to eat in the large formal dining room full of white cloth and leaded crystal. The men and women who worked for them sat and ate too. Conversation flowed in Irish and English. Donald sat next to Finney, their relationship continued where Lucas left off.

Finney sat and thought of his dead friend Lucas, all they did over the years together, and all he did since Lucas died. He thought of his wives and his parents.

Lucas believed everything anyone told him about spirits and superstition and religion.

Lucas believing what was not a victory or too reassuring. He believed every tale the Mexicans, the Spaniards, and the Indians told him. The priests too. "If he hadn't been a cheap son of a bitch," Finney had told Donald more than once, "he would have given all his money away on tall tales and pronouncements from shaman, medicine men, truth seers and priests."

Donald inherited his grandfather's fascination with cultural superstition and phenomena but did not react to them in the passionate way Lucas had.

"You going back over after we eat?"

"I should, there's a lot of checking to be done. Melinda and I need to go through the Memorial Museum building for Mister de Young. Earlier today we were looking over one of the buildings we contracted for them and Missus de Young stopped to chat."

"How did they fare in the disaster, at home?" Finney asked.

"No one was hurt. It spared their houses. They have damage at the main house but she told Melinda their water and gas still functioned. She said there are some large cracks in a few of the museum's walls. Melinda told her we would stop by later and look things over for her. Did not sound like they had much faith the city would prioritize the safety of the collections."

"Margie decided the cameos need to go to a museum and I think she settled on Mister de Young's. While you're there look and see how that wing or addition or whatever I'm paying to build for them is progressing. Hope there's not too much quake damage on the new work." Smiling he added, "If it's a loss we'll name it for the Pritchards, if it's okay I'll keep it named for the McCurrens and the Pritchards."

Donald smiled at the tired man's old humor.

"I'll do it Finney. How many cameos do you think you own?"

"There are about fifteen from my mother and the families of my poor dead wives. Margie has four or five from her mother and aunties. Then there's the few hundred I bought over the years."

He took a sip of his tall whiskey.

"I few hundred?" Donald asked incredulously.

He stared at Finney.

"I like buying them. They're small and pretty and each one depicts a tale. The women I've loved adored them. I never meant to buy so many. Whenever I saw a new one at a store, like the City of Paris or a hawk shop, I just bought it. I have two dealers who buy them for me sight-unseen and ship them over.

“I got a bunch made over the years too. Hell, I had one made for Estelle, my second poor wife, with a U.S. Marshal's badge on the back. A small star in a circle with the words around the edges. I got one for each wife and child carved in shell or ivory. They have precious stones embedded in them. Mounted in gold and white gold and silver with filigree and such. One at a time they are nice but when seen all together they're a pretty impressive bunch.”

Donald wiped his mouth with the starched linen napkin, “I'm sure they are. Is there a known value for them?”

“Hell boy, a couple are worth a few hundred thousand just in the stones alone. One is kinda ugly but made out of gold my father dug out near Sutter's with his own hands. They're worth enough to get into the museum and out of my safes. I could use the extra room in the safes. I want a little card next to each one noting the jeweler, who it's a likeness of, the materials and date created. Each one tells a story in its appearance, in a scene or likeness. Each one is a story in its history too, in its providence, materials, craftsman, and past owners.”

“Why cameos. Why not cufflinks or guns or watches,” Donald asked, fork in hand.

“I collect all those too. Women are more likely to kiss you when you give them jewelry than when you buy yourself cufflinks or give them a timepiece. Especially if the jewelry carries a likeness of some bible story or Greek God or their Mama or Auntie or Baby. Or horse. Estelle loved the one with her favorite mare's likeness. Large stones cleverly cast with precious metal always warrant a lot of kissing and such.”

“Yes it does,” Donald agreed, “yes it does.”

Supper over, the families adjourned to the recreation

rooms of the house. I cleaned, oiled, and polished all the firearms we could find. Baths and the reading of many stories preceded the small children, including Aidan, going to bed. The baby, fed and swaddled, slept in a crib in the nursery far from exterior walls and windows. Margie and Finney, Abigail and James, Melinda and Donald, and Angela gathered on the porch to watch the smoke rise from the city and the boats continue moving people back and forth across the bay. The wind blew hot from the sea and moved most of the smoke toward the Land of the Oaks and the tall hot hills.

The staff of three houses made short work of the cleanup. They assembled supplies for the refugee camps in the city's parks, specifically the Ashbury Heights area surrounding the Avenue Drive, in large quantity. The kitchen in each guest cottage glowed with yellow electric light. Music came from the bay side of the great house onto the porch, lawn and shore.

They placed telephone calls checking on friends, business, and damage to surrounding areas and ordered telegraphs to the otherwise unreachable.

"I am told we shall have quite the large and delicious breakfast," Angela said with smoke curling from her mouth. "If the three cooks don't kill one another it should come off very nicely."

Charles rolled another cigarette for Finney, "If I had it to do again I would expand the main kitchen even further and make it larger. Seems like we inevitably wind up using the cottage kitchens."

Finney struck a kitchen match and cupped the flame in his hands. The others watched as he lit his little hand rolled cigarette in the wind from the bay.

"How do you do that?" Charles asked, "Will you

show me?"

"Muslim fellow from over about North Africa taught me that a long time ago in the Sierras. It's wind-proof and hard to see from far away. Helps a man in rough country avoid shots fired or stalking. You strike the match holding it between your pointer finger and thumb," Finney pretended to strike the match.

"Then you hold the lit tip down near the meat of your hand, so the flame almost touches the base of your ring finger, but not close enough to burn. Then you cup the palm of your other hand to the space around the burning match like so, making a wind guard. Poke the end of your cigar through the circle of your pointer finger and thumb holding the match. Light up. Only trick is not to burn yourself."

Charles did as instructed while the others watched. He lit his rolled cigarette, facing the bay, with one match.

"I spoke to the honorable Governor Pardee," Finney said. "Claims the federal boy are gonna to be stingy on reconstruction by the public sector but the state would probably be able to compensate pretty close to ninety eight cents on the dollar. He also said he would make some calls to friends of his with lumber yards and see who he could put me in touch with."

James smiled, "That's great Finney. Donald and Melinda are heading back across. We must have at least another hour of daylight and then the museum will have something to light their way I'm sure." He looked at his gold watch. "In fact, I think I'll join them."

He left the porch and walked down to the pier. Angela followed and took hold of his coat sleeve. He turned to her with a look of interruption and question on his face.

"You come back here smelling like whore and you'll

be sleeping on the boat. Hear me?"

He laughed, gave he a peck on her cheek, "You're the only whore for me my darling."

Drink in hand he turned and walked away. He strolled down to the pier and hopped on deck without looking back. A tear formed in her eye and she willed it not to fall. On board and portside, studying the city and the bay, Donald turned and said, "Do you remember what you told me the night I married Melinda?"

"Something obscene I'm sure," James answered.

"Yes, something obscene. Also, something true. It was the end of the evening. We were walking to the carriage. They were all ahead of us and you had your arm around my shoulders. You gripped my shoulder hard in your hand and said, clearly, "Keep her well-sexed and you will keep her happy." It turns out to be true. And to work both ways."

"And what is your point my boy? Are you using my own advice against me now?" James grinned.

"I am."

"Well your mother and I have grown apart. At least physically. She prefers what I consider boring. I now appreciate what she considers nasty."

James spat into the black water. The yacht, loaded with supplies and her three passengers pulled away from the pier.

"I don't know, father. Melinda is privy to many of her conversations with Angela and, I blush to say so, but Mother misses you."

James stared at his son.

"Are you telling your father how to be a husband?"

Donald stared into James's face.

"I am telling you both that you are miserable and

lonely even when together and apparently have nothing to do with each other outside unhidden contempt and pride. I am advising you to treat your wife as if you love her. You should at least attempt to enjoy each other again if possible. Before there is no turning back for either of you."

Donald turned away and strolled below.

James closed his eyes. He felt the salty spray on his face. The crystal glass slipped from his grasp and plunked into the bay. "Damn."

Chapter Seventeen

The small craft lurched and rocked as they tacked almost to the mouth of the bay. The skipper turned the vessel before the rocks hidden at the mouth of the Pacific Ocean, the dreaded Potato Patch. They sailed to the landing and loaded a waiting wagon with the sandwiches and blankets and casks of water and sacks of buns and biscuits. James and Curtis Oliver drove the supplies to the Avenue Drive refugee camp. Donald, Melinda, and Bobby Watson, shotgun across his lap rode in a smaller faster cabriolet. Donald navigated across the top of the city and down through the center skirting the Presidio Reservation and the central cemeteries.

Melinda clutched Donald's arm as they passed Masonic Cemetery.

"Oh Donald," she said.

He slowed the buggy and they watched a gang of small grimy children chase a little dog though the cemetery. Most of the children carried sticks while others threw stones at the mangy dog. Obviously looking for an escape, the headstones and the large iron fence confused the cur. Bobby Watson raised the large shotgun from his lap, shouldered the stock, and said, "Cover your ears."

He fired into the air and the children stopped in their tracks. The dog spied his escape and ran to the gates at the street entrance.

Bobby hollered at the cemetery urchins, "Where you mama's and papa's?"

A reply came back in a boy's high voice, "They dead."

Another voice, a girl's said, "They got squished in the bed by the chimbley. It fell on them hard."

Bobby Watson asked, "What's their name then?"

The boy said, "Janice and Evan Reiter."

Bobby thought. Then he said, "They're not dead. I seen 'em this morning at the Avenue Drive camp. They were lookin' for you kids though. Get on out of there and down to Avenue Drive before I come in and get you and march you there myself and tell your mama and your papa what you been doin' up here. Those dead people have problems enough without a bunch of wild kids running around atop of them."

Each child stared at its feet. A smaller boy began crying and the girl who spoke before refused to move.

"I ain't walkin' on dead people," she cried, "I ain't walkin' on nobody."

They refused to budge.

Bobby Watson left his gun in the cabriolet, entered the cemetery and walked to where the frightened children stood.

"What do you think this place is? Each of these blocks stands for a dead person laid deep below the ground. I'm standing on two dead people, see? There's the names: Robert and Harriet Culpepper. Oh! Look! Says they died on the day of the big one in eighteen sixty-eight. This is bad! Oh my Lord God! We gotta get out of here and quick, this is bad! All you go! Get on outta here."

He scooped up the petrified little girl and ran with her over one shoulder behind the pack of little kids. They screamed and streamed out of the cemetery gate to the street and down the hill. He placed the bawling child on her feet. She recovered her bearings quickly and ran after her friends, calling to them all the way. Bobby Watson laughed as he pulled the gate shut and wrapped the chain around the fence and gate. He secured the chain high on the wrought iron out of the reach of little kids.

He hopped into the buggy and smiled.

"Who are Robert and Harriet Culpepper?" Melinda asked, "Not two victims of the eighteen sixty eight quake?"

"Nope," Bobby Watson grinned, "They're my Ma's people, the Culpeppers are. They live over on Cole Street. All my kin are Odd Fellow and Rebekahs. Wouldn't be caught dead or alive in a Masonic cemetery."

The drove down the hill and gaped at the destruction. Families sat on their possessions, rolled mattresses and random chairs, cooking supper over fires made from dressers and broken tables, doors and shattered window frames.

Military personnel and police officers stood on every corner. Donald stopped each block and showed their passes written earlier in the day by Mayor Schmitz. At the edge of the park, the National Guard's men were also cooking dinner and lining refugees up to collect their supper ration. Bobby Watson scanned the crowd naming friends and neighbors as he happily recognized faces. Donald and Bobby Watson wore deputy U.S. Marshal Badges. Each was armed and held his pass to the officers who asked for verification of open passage.

"What's your work here, young man?" A burly and clean-shaven bulldog of a Marine sergeant asked Donald.

"I'm a builder; we are here to inspect the Memorial Museum for the city and the de Young's."

The sergeant stood taller, "Very good, sir. Mister de Young arrived just a moment ago, as did the head curate. They were anxious I send you on immediately. I trust you know the way. Please proceed cautiously; there are a few fallen power poles my men removed from the drive. Surprisingly many still have power, as does the museum. Just show your passes to the men at its entrance."

Donald thanked the sergeant and drove on.

In the park, Bobby Watson kept the shotgun standing, ready to fall to attention. Occasional surviving electric lights lit their way into the park through the turns to the grounds of the Memorial Museum. Melinda looked about and shivered. The sun was setting and the heavy trees cooled the air.

"I love this park. I cannot believe how lucky we are to have it in our city. I still get lost in it."

Bobby Watson agreed, "I do too. I like riding near the far end close to the ocean where you can hear the surf but can't see anything but trees and lawn and the trail you're on."

The horse pulled them up to the front of the Memorial Museum. They left the buggy next to a fine salon with a liveried driver and two massive black horses being brushed by a small groom.

Police officers, Pinkertons, and military personnel swarmed around the building. A crew of workers stood near wagons waiting for something to do. Donald and Melinda, trailed by Bobby Watson and his huge shotgun, approached to the front entrance of the museum and presented their credentials to the man there.

A gruff police officer in a stiff dark uniform took the proffered papers and grunted looking at Bobby Watson.

"Who's this then? He cannot bring that weapon in here. It shouldn't even be in the park."

Bobby Watson flinched. Slowly showing his badge he replied, "I'm Deputy United States Marshal Robert Watson. I'm on the city's payroll as a guard for city supervisor James Pritchard and his family. I'm also a licensed Pinkerton out of the San Francisco office. Who the fuck are you, then, mate?"

Bobby gripped the shotgun across his chest ready to

slam the stock into the man's face if necessary.

The officer started and said, “If you are entering this building you cannot bring any weapons. If you chose to remain outside you will have to stay next to your buggy.”

Bobby Watson began to speak, white knuckles gripping his weapon. Donald placed a hand on his arm, “Hold on Bobby Watson.”

To the officer he said, “There is no way you are getting our weapons from us. Not today. The de Young's are waiting for us and we do not have time to mess with this. Please tell Mister de Young we were here and we were denied entrance.”

To Melinda and Bobby Watson he said, “Let's go. Don't kill him Bobby, please? Let's just go.”

Bobby relaxed, “Okay.”

The silent Pinkerton who was standing by said, “Give 'em a God damn break would you Smitty. You heard the man say he was a Goddamn deputy U.S. Marshal and a Pinkerton. You see both the men have badges. What are you going for here? If not for this gent and his Missus, the Pinkerton woulda smashed your face with the butt of that shotgun and we all would have said you had it coming. The de Young's are here to see these folks so shut yer yap and pass 'em on in. Guns and all.”

To the three visitors, “Do us a favor then; no shooting up the art. Okay folks?”

“Thank you,” Donald said.

The officer blushed and Bobby Watson bumped him hard enough with his shoulder as he passed to knock him into the thick brown adobe wall of the museum.

Donald produced a notebook from a pocket and began sketching each wall of the entrance area.

Melinda said, "I see the curator, I'll go speak with him."

Bobby Watson asked, "You want me with you or her?"

Donald looked up from his pad of notes uncomprehending for a moment and removed a pencil from his mouth.

"You mind shadowing her, Bobby? I have a pistol but I cannot imagine anyone is going to have trouble up here. She's unarmed but the de Young's people are known to be bumbling city morons like that clown out front."

Bobby Watson agreed and turned to follow Melinda. She stood in the main gallery speaking to an older, distinguished gentleman. Medium height with short-cropped gray hair, he wore a dark suit and grave, chiseled expression. Three private guards stood further off. Bobby Watson knew each of them as off-duty city officers.

Each looked at the shotgun in Bobby's hands and smiled.

"I spoke to Finney McCurren. He and Margie McCurren, his wife, decided to donate the entire collection of cameos to the museum. My husband Donald spoke to Finney further and he's curious about the status of the new gallery wing the McCurren's are financing."

The curate smiled and clasped his hands to his chest, said, "It looks to me like the damage was minimal but we'll need Bobby to thoroughly inspect the more hidden areas with the rest of the building."

He waved his hands around, surprising Melinda and the guards and himself exclaiming, "The cameos will be brilliant! Oh my, the de Young's will be excited. The McCurrens have always been a fine family, a credit to the city."

Melinda smiled, "Yes I suppose they have."

Donald joined them.

"I need to get into the roof area and the space between the walls."

Stephen Mills, the curate said, "Of course, come with me, won't take but a minute."

They followed him out of the main gallery and down a corridor.

"There are access doors all over the building but I'll take you to the anti-chamber. It provides the easiest entrance to both the ceiling structure and the display walls."

Walking behind the two men Bobby asked Melinda, "What are they talking about?"

"The facade of the museum is a just that: A fake shell. Adobe and large wooden beams form the walls and a series of large glass windows carpet the roof for naturally lighting the galleries. The building material used for the construction of the outside is not the best for displaying and lighting the work inside. It is a unique and beautiful building but if the galleries followed the outline of the exterior walls, the flow of the collections might feel choppy and disconnected.

"With so many works and so many different needs for each display a system is in place where the museum workers may manipulate the walls and ceiling. Accommodating the layout and the lighting of each piece or group of pieces displayed. They rotate the collection so often that after a few years, if they used the actual exterior support walls, the framing and plaster would just simply crumble. Therefore, the walls in the galleries are facades.

She rapped on a wall with her knuckles to illustration her point. The wall sounded deep, heavy, and hollow.

"They have crawl spaces behind them. The ceilings are facades too. A twenty-foot ceiling swallows a display of ancient figurines but is essential for huge wall tapestries or old portraits. A series of catwalks and ladders above us allow access and more or less natural light from the roof windows as needed."

"Is that why everything here looks okay? I mean, there appears to be no damage at all," Bobby asked.

"Exactly," Donald agreed with Melinda's summary.

"These walls and ceilings don't do anything but facilitate the display of the collection. I need to crawl around behind and above them to look at the real walls and ceiling to assess what damage, if any, was sustained."

Stephen Mills the curate added, "The walls are two feet thick in some places so we usually fare pretty well with the smaller quakes. We added so many galleries in such a short amount of time. We have some structures built inside others and we have different ceilings and basements. It gets confusing and hard to remember why what was done when, even only a few months after work is completed."

Donald agreed.

"The real solution is to tear the entire museum down and build one large fantastic facility that won't be outgrown for a long, long time."

The curate said, "That is as unrealistic as trying to get all these smaller areas to be the same quality and consistency. I suppose if they built an entirely new museum somewhere else the collections could be moved in and this structure could be torn down and rebuilt or be put into use for some other purpose."

Melinda said, "The park location is half the majesty and beauty of the museum."

"Alas," Stephen Mills agreed with a sigh.

He removed a heavy ring of bit-keys from his pocket and unlocked a large heavy wooden door. They entered an office. It looked like a cyclone had hit, with crates lining every wall and reams of papers littering one large desk.

"Please pardon the mess," Stephen said, "Sometimes brilliance takes a disordered appearance and a very long time to run its eventual brilliant and orderly course."

He cleared wood crates and straw away from a second large door. He unlocked it with a key from the same large ring. The door stuck, he pulled the large brass knob energetically with both hands eventually opening the way. The door opened on creaking hinges to reveal a damp and dusty wall space that looked like the neglected root cellar of an ante-bellum house.

Pipes ran every direction, the dark metal frame that secured lathe and plaster walls to the exterior wall and foundation competed for space with huge beams supporting the ceiling thirty feet above. Furry-looking electric wires coated with dust skirted steam pipes. Directions and notes, written by years of workers, were on the larger pipes in chalk or ran along the walls and floor along the skinnier pipes.

Donald screwed his hat on tighter, stuck his pad of papers into the back of his trousers, bit his pencil and began climbing the framing. In a moment, they heard him walking on the ceiling of the office above their heads. Bobby placed his shotgun in a corner, picked up a discarded ball of chalk and on a wide beam drew a five-pointed star in a circle. He scrawled "U.S. Marshal" above and "R.W. 1906" below.

Stephen Mills said, "Our newest acquisition to the hidden collection."

Bobby Watson smiled self-consciously and blushed

slightly.

Melinda smiled, “What is all this, Mister Mills?”

She gestured to the wooden crates and piles of straw. His eyes sprang and he again gesticulated excitedly.

“These are the Egyptian artifacts we have been cataloging for over seven months. They will initially be displayed in the McCurren gallery with the donation of the cameos.”

Cautiously he asked, “Did Mister McCurren happen to mention how many pieces constitute the donation?”

“Finney mentioned a few hundred valued over a few million dollars.”

“Oh my,” Stephen Mills said clasping and unclasping his hands again, “Oh my, indeed.”

They heard another bump and Bobby Watson asked, “How can he see up there, are there electric bulbs?”

“Yes,” Stephen Mills replied, “A series of electric lights illuminate the entire area. Otherwise, it is quite dark, especially in the evening. We complete a large amount of the museum's maintenance at night to accommodate uninterrupted access to the collections by our patrons during the day. The entire upper area is lit with electric light.”

Donald walked along wooden catwalk made of twin horizontal beams and skinny perpendicular slats. Suspended from the roof, all was supported by unfinished redwood struts that filled hands and fingers with fine splinters at the slightest touch. He examined each intersection and join of wood. He looked at or touched each corner where walls met or ceiling intersected wall. The large sky windows made him uneasy when he crossed below them. The panes were huge and heavy. He had no idea if they would fall on him. He added enlisting a glazier for a thorough inspection to the growing list of tasks.

At the gallery designed and contracted for Finney he stooped and crawled through a joint where old adobe joined new concrete. The walls were thick and strong. Before pouring the foundations, footings, and enormous walls, they had fingered samples of the aggregate in large buckets. The little rocks were beautiful. Brought down by barge from a riverbed north of the city each small rock and pebble was an explosion of color when wet. As the water had dried on the rocks in his hands, their color faded to a uniform dullness of gray or dry red or black. Now the little stones managed to hold his walls in place through one of the hardest and longest quakes recorded in California. He considered the strength in the small stones, amazed.

Above the center of the gallery, he inspected steam pipes, water pipes, and the lengths of steel that secured the great ornate plaster and glass ceilings below. Finney hated the open spaces above and around the gallery. His idea was to build a very large vault with armed guards securing the collections within from theft and view. When he finally capitulated to the façade of walls and ceiling and the basements below, he requested booby traps "to keep the unimaginative larcenists on their God damn toes".

"He got them," Donald said to nobody as he stopped and retrieved his pocketknife from a deep pocket. He worked out a long splinter lodged in the meat of his right palm.

Months before the museum carpenters told him of a man, a boy really, who apprenticed with them in the early days. He was joining lengths of a new façade wall together in one of the larger galleries. With so many repetitive little tasks to complete he soon lost track of the time.

When the crews went home for the night, the lights

were extinguished, the busy fellow forgotten in complete darkness. He had no way of climbing out without one of the large sharp wires that held the wall to the bracing poking him in the face. The skinny wall made maneuvering or sitting in the dark impossible.

After a few hours, he got very cold due to the adobe he was pressed against and the chill of the night air from outside. His legs began to cramp. He was hungry and needed to relieve himself.

He located his tool bag on the floor and slowly fingered a hammer up into his hand. With small taps, he began knocking a hole in the interior wall. He swung harder and harder making the hole larger. He felt the warm air. It flowed into the space around him warming his chilled body. As the hole became larger, he was able to sit with his legs in the gallery, his bottom on the hole, his hammer slowly taping the gap out so he might turn and slide out without tearing up his backside.

The night guard, however, heard his banging. He alerted the station guards. Ten armed men walked the galleries as quietly as they could, listening to locate the banging. When they found its source, they also spied the man's legs dangling from a hole near the base of a wall full of seventeenth century Italian portraits.

Assuming they caught a very stupid thief in the middle of an imbecilic entry to the portrait gallery, the guards quietly waited and watched the man turn to climb out of his hole. When he did they noticed the leather belt around his waist and saw what they thought were explosives with the tools for breaking into their museum. One of the guards, timid and inexperienced, let his fingers slip, firing his weapon at the thief. The other guards fired too, assuming their thief was firing at them.

They killed the carpenter in the portrait gallery. When he was quite dead, they approached and turned the dusty and bloody body over. They recognized the funny new carpenter at once. Spying his tool bag and the hammer in his clenched lifeless fist, they knew what happened and understood what they had done in their fear, in the dark, with all those dead Italians watching.

Splinter removed, Donald walked the entire area before he descended into the wall next to the façade of the gallery's main entrance. He skirted the spaces in the walls thinking of the dead carpenter. Frequent wooden-framed ladders and easily accessible large switches to light each area lined wall cavities of this gallery. His inspection of the walls and foundation complete, Donald headed back up a ladder, maneuvered to the main catwalk and proceeded back the way he had come. He carefully avoided additional splinters. In the small office, Donald reported his findings to Stephen Mills. The new gallery had no damage. The older galleries had some small cracks they could address over the coming weeks.

In the buggy, they proceeded out of the park and through Ashbury Heights. They ran down Carl Street so Bobby Watson could check in on his own family. The Watson's were fine. They were sitting down to a cold supper lit by candles and old railroad lanterns. Hugs, kisses and brisk handshakes done, the three quickly made their way to the house on Buena Vista Avenue.

Chapter Twenty

Along the Avenue Drive James Prichard and Curtis Oliver distributed supplies and bags of food to the displaced citizens of Ashbury Heights. James received reports from the men he left in charge. They reported no incidents of looting or any other crimes. The thugs he paid to leave his voters in peace had so far kept to themselves. The National Guard, the regular troops, and local law enforcement spent their time attending to the legitimate needs of the citizenry, not chasing criminals or suppressing lawlessness. The Mayor's Shoot To Kill Act helped keep Ashbury Height's stubborn felons in line.

In the tent city, children rocked to sleep in the arms of tired parents and grandparents. Couples settled down, families counted their children and tied their tent flaps to keep out the chill, and keep older kids inside. James Pritchard had Curtis Oliver drive him to one of the only bawdy houses in town still open. Sitting in the wagon, parked out front, he watched familiar men approach and enter by the front stairs. Every other house on the block was silent and dark.

"Let's move on tonight, Curtis Oliver. I want to see Laurence on Buena Vista Avenue before he runs back to his fire and possibly gets his head staved in by a falling building or burning timber."

Curtis turned the long wagon and proceeded back to Ashbury Heights.

"You married Curtis?"

Curtis Oliver shook his head. "I was engaged once when I was young. I tried to marry a Cuban girl I fell in love with when we were over there. Mostly I don't meet women a man wants to introduce 'round to his mother and sisters and aunties."

"How's that?" James asked.

"Well, me and the lads mostly meet servant women and washer women and house maids. I don't have much idle time and that what I do have I spend drinking at the Green Hag. Few bar maids there won't rub your tummy for a bit of change. I spend my leisure time at the bawdy house and no girls there want to meet my Ma or aunties or sisters. A few probably already know my Pa. All the legal secretaries and women at the courthouse are already married. It's hard to find a nice woman anywhere other than church. The women I meet at church want to wait until after the knot's been tied to let a man see what's in their drawers."

"I guess it's hard to commit when you don't know what you're getting yourself into."

"That's what I used to think. Lately I've been wondering if it's true. A wife is a woman to love and maybe raise babies with you. A woman to have regular adult relations with at will. What I've been a wondering lately is what if they're to love and to share one mind with you? And the adult relations come and go? No trick in a man or woman gettin' a lay. maybe a wife, a church wife or a real woman a fellow learns to love, is more for being with after the romp is no longer a man's or woman's priority. As in the way you and Laurence always tell us to save our money for when we're old and unpaid because we'll be too feeble to earn.

"Maybe a wife, or a husband, is an old folk's savings. Except instead of money, you save experiences and familiarity. Maybe you save thoughts and kindred feelings. Maybe you can also romp to your heart's delight, assuming you ain't too old to get the Old Boy standing."

Curtis Oliver smiled, "God knows old Finney keeps coming up with more wives. Each prettier and finer the one before. Not that he prefers the tragedy of his past spouses. Don't take me wrong. He's the one told me before they left for the honeymoon his fourth wife's the same age he remembers the other three."

James said, "Finney told me the same thing. He has a thing for forty-year-old women. Best age for women, he says, because they have what they want in life or they know what they want in life.

"That is pretty much what he said to me too," Curtis Oliver agreed. "Maybe I'll call on the girl I been talking-up at church. Getting married couldn't hurt too much. At least it is surely something I never done before. Doing what I never done before has proved a pretty good rule to abide."

"Should be a commandment: "Thou shalt embrace the unknown and take up with the unfamiliar opportunities afforded by an active existence."

James asked, "What about a man who finds himself bored with his wife and now thinks she's tired of him too. What do I do if she's as done with me as I once thought I was with her? Other men want to be with her. Am I wasting all my time paying young women to do with me what I could be doing in my own house for the rest of my life with my own wife?

"I don't mind her stepping out. I started it and, God knows, not in moderation. What if the shortcoming I thought I saw in her never existed except in my own perception? Do I just tell her, "I'm done messing around, can we start messing around again together?"

"I think the secret to your situation," Curtis Oliver said as they rounded the base of the park and began the uphill approach to the houses on Buena Vista Avenue, "Is to just make the changes but don't acknowledge them. Giving countenance to past indiscretion through admission, no matter what she says, will only lead to misery, pain, and some large fights.

"You don't want to know what she's been up to. She doesn't want to know what you've been up to. What's important in a situation like yours is to play the game of blissful ignorance until the ignorance is gone through renewed familiarity and bliss is left. Just start being around. She likes to drink. They all do. Carry her off to bed some night when you're both sozzled and, if you'll pardon the familiarity, make it a new evening habit. Sozzled or not."

James studied Curtis Oliver.

"You're sure you've never been married?"

"Nope," Curtis Oliver said, "over the years I've shared in plenty of indiscretions with women who were married though."

James stared at him and he quickly added, "No one you know, no one you know." They laughed.

Atop Buena Vista Avenue, they found the men on the porches of the two houses. They listened to the night, smoked, and drank small glasses of tepid dark beer. Donald and Melinda's buggy stood at the curb, a young boy was brushing their ravenous horse. Long wagon parked and the horses left in the care of the groom, James and Curtis Oliver crossed the road. James took the steps two at a time and entered his house. Curtis Oliver joined his partner. They shared a beer, rolled lengths of tobacco, and spoke of what each had done since they parted ways at the landing earlier.

Inside James changed his suit and gathered a few items forgotten by his wife. He heard laughter come from the house next door, the house of his best friend and family. Nostalgia gripped him as he gathered his kit and recalled the sounds from the house next door as a boy. The sounds of his best friend, the family and the people he loved like his own. His father, Lucas Pritchard and Finney McCurren had, it seemed, always known each other. He and Laurence grew up steeped in their stories and molded by the memories of these two strong men born and raised in the wilds of California when there were more Spaniards and Natives than Europeans.

Finney and Lucas took the boys into the woods and around the bay fishing and hunting at every chance. They taught them to respect other men and women, to clean a gun, tan leather, and put a razor edge on any knife. They taught them to cook camp food. The value of money and the value of keeping it. How to dance and how to speak to a woman, a lady, a mistress. They taught them to how to ride, how to sail, how to tell stories, and how to fight. They taught them how to smoke, curse, and drink, how to gamble and how to cheat. Encouraging at every turn, they taught their boys an enthusiasm for their lives and the life of their families. Later Lucas and Finney taught them how to wrangle at politics in a hidden kind of sleight of hand that got what they wanted done and kept graft and greed in check as much as was safe or prudent. They taught their boys responsibility and that there are always choices in life and not making your choice is a choice in itself. Usually more wrong than any of the lesser options ignored or disregarded.

James took the stairs down two at a time. Excited like a boy he leaped the porch, ran down the walk and bounded up the McCurren porch. He was with his friends at the large servant's table in the kitchen before the bottle made another pass. Laurence McCurren, tall and broad, strong and clean, sat laughing at one end with James's grown son Donald and his lovely, brilliant wife Melinda. The guards the family employed for years, the skinny and odd Bobby Watson and his partner Curtis Oliver, handsome and easy with either a woman or a loaded pistol, sat too.

He ran into the kitchen and hollered. They stood and yelled too. Laurence handed him the bottle and he took a long slow drink that cooled his throat and evaporated from the heat of his own body on his neck and chest as it dribbled from his chin. Bobby Watson handed him a thin hand rolled cigar and someone pushed a plate of warm rabbit stew with crumbly chunks of bread in front of his chair. This was his life. From small boy with short pants and skinned knees drinking milk with his best pal and his father and mother, to his best pal and his own grown son with his wife and two men he was proud to call friends and with whom he trusted the lives of those he cherished.

"Rabbit stew?" He asked genuinely surprised. "Is Finney McCurren here? Or the ghost of a hungry Lucas Pritchard?"

They laughed and Laurence said, "The hungry ghost of that son of a bitch is always in my kitchen according to my old man, but the stew was made by Bobby Watson here, earlier today. The bread came from his family. Strong soda bread for a strong soda kind of day."

James looked at Bobby Watson who smiled, "I found myself looking down the sight of a rifle at a one-eared coney earlier. I took advantage of my position on the porch and at the house to dress my kill and boil this fine critter up in Finney's fashion."

They all smiled as Laurence said, "You mean you boiled her in as much whiskey as water? Taking a slug for yourself each time you stirred the pot? So regardless of how fine or poorly it cooked up you could believe it was perfect by the time it was ready to eat?"

Bobby Watson nodded, "Ain't that what I just said? Welsh rarebit improved only by a heartier mirepoix than Finney is usually able to throw together. I found fennel bulbs in Cook's garden."

They laughed and tucked into the meal. The tepid dark beer was uncasked into small pitchers. They took turns drinking from the bottle of whiskey and refilling their plates with Welsh rarebit. And refilling their glasses with the earthy porter.

Laurence asked, "How do you suppose that hare came to have just one ear?"

He looked down the table at his friend.

Bobby Watson replied, "It looked freshly shot off. No telling what happened, or even where that ear is. Somewhere in the park, I figure."

"Thom McCurren shot it off this very morning. Shot it off from ten yards with a rifle from that automobile we took down to the fire line. I lost a fiver on that shot but he kept me from paying it to Edgar Pepper."

James smiled a small smile. Bobby Watson and Curtis Oliver stopped eating and looked at one another.

Laurence said, "He told me all about Edgar Pepper and the coney's ear. He also told me about his quick deputy's oath and badge ceremony."

Laurence wiped the corners of his mouth with a white cotton napkin.

James chewed and said, "Thomas saved me today. Edgar had it in mind to follow me into the house and Thomas, just by being here and then by distraction up the road, gave me the chance I needed to get over on Edgar

Pepper. I made sure it was as legitimate and lawful as possible. I didn't have time to fill the boy in on Edgar's details."

James took a bite of bread.

Laurence asked, "He doesn't know about Finney and the governor and why the governor sent Edgar Pepper to us?"

James replied, "He's smart, Thom is. He knew what was going on when he saw Edgar's face as we entered the house. Thom discerned the cut of his jib without any help from me. Too much talk would have made both of us nervous and Edgar Pepper would have caught onto us conspiring, as well."

"He acted like himself and all went well. Do not be cross with me, please. He noticed everything I was doing, everything I was watching. He sure noticed Edgar's interests. I was proud of him and told him so."

James tore another chunk of bread from the shrinking loaf.

"Today was a day of surprises and no one was more surprised than I to be throwing my Godson in with the wolves. I didn't make the quake or the fire and I'm not solely responsible for the caliber of associates we regularly meet while safeguarding our families and neighborhood. Edgar Pepper was your father's responsibility. Perhaps it's fitting his grandson was involved in rounding out that responsibility. Besides, Laurence, you were off fighting fires."

Laurence continued to stare at his best friend.

James rested his spoon on the table.

"What do you suppose I should have done? What was Thom supposed to do? I had to get the capital to secure the hands we need to rebuild and to buy off the men who otherwise would be tearing through every Ashbury Heights house still standing. Edgar knew my timeframe. He knew my objective. He knew I had the capital at hand or I would have been sweating and scheming my way to a downtown bank. Dismissing him or reassigning him would have tipped my hand. Would have shown what I suspected. What we all suspected.

"Thom was my partner today and he did right by me. The way you and I taught him, each of them, to do. The way Finney and Lucas and our Mama's taught us."

James drained his glass of beer.

Laurence studied his hands, "We should be talking about where we stand for tomorrow and Thom should be here if he is going to start taking a lead role in our responsibilities. Donald tells me we're ready to start pouring foundations as soon as the wreckage is sorted and cleared."

They heard a buggy and horse and then the two baby-faced brigade sergeants were standing at the door of the large kitchen.

"Grab a bowl and seat boys," Laurence said standing.

He retrieved two more glasses and poured them full of the dark bubbly beer. He then poured two fingers of whiskey into the glasses and handed them to the tired men who stank of sweat and close burning.

"What news?" Laurence asked as they all sat again and the sergeant's buttered chunks of bread and greedily lay into the piping rabbit stew.

"They still have no idea what to do without Sully down their coordinating everything. We kept our sections covered and cleared but there are so many pumps out and mains broken it's hard to imagine we can do much more to contain the blaze without help from the sea."

The sergeant took another heaping spoonful as the other sergeant took up where he left off,

"Bastards from the reserves tried to take us off the position you left us on. I told him we could only retreat or flank if by a direct order from you or one of your superiors. Looked like he was gonna shoot me. Then the Father,"

"Auxiliary Bishop Augustine?"

"That's our Father. He gave us a lift back to the front as you instructed with the supplies and stayed to help. He sorted the wounded for a while. In fact, I had forgotten all about him. Then the reservists came up on us. Their man was telling us to move. Telling how many of our brigade he would be commandeering when the Father walked up. He looked at the little priest and stopped shouting. The Father said, "Take your men and move off son. You're wasting your breath on my boys."

"And you know, we all are kinda his boys. We were going over it later and he either baptized or gave first communion or married or did all too almost all of us in the brigade.

"So the Father tells him to move off and your man looks like the all the roads heading south out of town: No way San Jose."

"The whole time the Father is winding his purple sacrament around his hand like a prize fighter fixing to lace gloves on. The man from the reserves opens his mouth to speak and the Father right hooks him in his face. The man's nose popped. We all heard it pop like an electric light bulb tossed in the air hitting the ground. Which is exactly what he did after the father, while everyone watched, stunned, punched him in the mouth hard enough to break teeth and cut one of the Father's fingers to the bone. He was wearing one of them huge gold Holy See rings too. The reservist went down on his knees and fell to the side. The Father glared at his prey and then at the troops, who by now were pointing their rifles at him.

"He inflated and rose. I swear. Rose off his feet into the air seething in anger."

"And began laying into them with more filth mixed in with holy Latin and holy oaths of promised personal visits to Satan than anyone ever heard at the worst of drunken Italian whore houses. We grabbed our Father and kept him from throwing himself on their bayoneted rifles. They lowered their guns and collected their fallen man. We kept the Father from kicking the unconscious fellow. A medic attended to the Father's hand. The man stained the Father's purple sacraments with his crusted blood and snot. We put him in his buggy and rode back here to fetch you. He's passed out in the back now with a bottle he fished from under his tunic."

Laurence rose and James asked, "He's outside now?"

"He was. Probably still is. Believe me he needs the rest. I think he might a snapped today. He took on a wild look like one of those orphans we keep coming across. Too scared to do anything but fight and tear at anyone they see."

Chapter Twenty One

Laurence and James ventured outside and located Auxiliary Bishop Augustus snoring in the back of his small black buggy. They corked his bottle and, each grabbing an arm, pulled him out and walked him up the porch and into the house. They carried him to an empty sitting room and arranged him languidly on a long red velvet divan.

Sneaking out of the room they heard the Father say, "I saved your brigade for you my boy. I feel stifled, is it hot in here? Stuffy? I am truly burning up."

James left. Laurence returned and crossed the room to open a pair of large wooden French doors. The breeze from the ocean billowed sheer lace curtains like confused ghosts.

Father Augustine opened one eye, "Much better my boy. Thank you so."

He quietly burped and paused. He quietly burped again.

"One indicator by which a man can tell he is old: the old man mystery burps. I sit in my study at the rectory and burp for no reason. Removing myself from the bath, I burp. Again for no reason. Do you burp mysteriously, Laurence McCurren?"

Laurence looked at the old priest, "No Father. I don't burp without cause. Finney does. Lucas Pritchard used to. He also got the hiccups pretty easily."

The Father sat up and slumped at one end of the divan.

"Much cooler in here already. Did I ever tell you of the parishioner, a woman, who hiccupped when possessed by an overwhelming desire for the touch of a man?"

Laurence chuckled expecting a joke.

"No messing," The small priest said weighing his swollen hand in the other. "This was a long time ago. I was a new priest in a new land and she was a young beauty of ample proportions. Unmarried but experienced. Of high birth. When she told me, I had no thought of what to tell her. Therefore, I never told her anything. At least nothing of value. I was a celibate. An inexperienced whelp of a boy. Here was a grown woman, perfect in every way, telling me her body ached for the caress of a man, for a woman's pleasure of a man, so hard she had a physical reaction to her unsated desire.

"It drove me mad for weeks. I would be standing in line to buy a loaf at the baker's and she would queue up somewhere behind me with her small, "hic, hic, hic." Crossing a street with some kindly wealthy matron with an intention of benefaction and I would hear, "hic, hic, hic" and know. And become embarrassingly distracted. Feel confused. She told me she successfully abused herself in multiple intense attempts to relieve the strain but never achieved the desired conclusion. Her hiccups became stronger each passing day, each successive week. I began having a small breakfast of bread and butter at a café near her house so I could clandestinely monitor the progress of her condition.

"Finally, one late afternoon, fate brought her to my door for an unrelated conversation. Her brother was going to war. Would I please come to the family's farewell dinner the following week? She sat next to me on a sofa much like this one and spoke with a small accented, "hic, hic, hic" peppering her speech. She told me things were worse. She could no longer sleep soundly due to her dreams of pleasure and the violence of her hiccups.

"She tried to seduce a local livery boy who was so

unnerved by her "hic, hic, hic" he was unable to rise to the occasion. She began to weep. She told me she was so distracted by her unfulfilled passion she began contemplating the sin of suicide. It was apparent in her face sleep was no longer her companion.

"So I kissed her. She gasped, hiccupped, and kissed me back in a manner I only ever heard about in the confessional. Before I knew, she was astride me. Her hiccups caused her to squeeze me so tightly with each "hic" I thought she might damage me in some peculiar way. The faster she moved the more frequently she hiccupped, "hic, hic, hic" until she wailed and they stopped.

"She seemed to drift as I cupped her large round breasts in the palms of my hands. She continued rocking on me slowly. I was stunned. I never before witnessed the ferocity of an uninhibited woman's pleasure and I was awed. Completely out to sea. "Out of my depth", as the sailors and merchantmen are fond of saying.

"As if reading my mind she swung her dark hair from her face and opened her mouth slightly. She burped. It swept me away. The most sensual creature I had ever touched or probably ever known and her small hard burp immediately illustrated in my mind the futility and the absurdity, the sin, if you will, of dogma and dichotomy. The fallacy of inhibiting the human animal of her and this God given, innocent and small burping pleasure, was so clearly absurd to me.

"I realigned my life in an instant. Perhaps it was the series of instances with her over the following years. There you have the moment in my life when I became a good priest and began to understand a human-sized quantity of the universe around me, my universe. With us here, traveling as the smallest and most insignificant specks on God's universe.

"That is also when I began fighting against sin disguised as dichotomy whenever and wherever encountered. This has been a day of dichotomy. A day of fighting. I met your oldest boy as a man for the first time today. Impressive. I used to think he had a lot to live up to, coming from you, Angela, Finney, and Caroline. I was wrong. You, Angela, and Finney have some catch up work to sweat out if you three are to maintain even the same pace as him. I liked him very much.

He looked around the room and heard the clatter from the kitchen.

"Where is Finney? I want the Pritchards and McCurrens to help me, the diocese rather, rebuild our church and hospital. I do not like the idea that they could fall around my families at a moment's notice. I had visions of the large cross on top of the spire being shaken from its moorings and plunging to the ground smiting one of my worse sinners while holding the hand of his or her unsuspecting lamb of a spouse. Not the best way to lose a loved one, even one so hateful as to be selected for cross-smiting by God's incidental shifting of our paradise next to the bay. James's Donald and Melinda are the engineers, correct?"

Laurence laughed, "I'm glad you are feeling more like yourself, Father. Yes, they're here. Yes, you do smell Welsh rarebit. Let's get a bowl. You can work out a plan with the Pritchards."

They rose from the velvet divan. Father August picked a bottle of whiskey up from a sideboard and carrying it to the kitchen, "We'll probably want for this."

He lumbered into the kitchen and blessed the diners. He found a saucer and a heavy silver spoon and helped himself to a large serving of Bobby Watson's Welsh rarebit.

Spying the beer, he also located a tall crystal glass and filled it to the top with the rich thick porter.

Seating himself next to Laurence, "Where's the house staff gone, buried in the cellar with the good port?"

They smiled and James reminded him of Charles's house across the bay. The Father began to eat then stopped in the petrified stares of Laurence's sergeants.

"Relax lads. The fist of God is bruised and battered. It shall not fly again until tomorrow morning. Even then I shall be taking care of my responsibilities at the church and leaving you to yours without a crazy old man attempting to get you each shot."

They stared harder.

"I am too tired and too drunk to pretend to be the mild mannered, passive clergy you and yours have convinced yourselves you need or should expect. Human beings are human beings regardless of their appearance, experience or status. If any one of us can ever honestly get a glimpse of God's Grace, we should all be truly amazed and sympathetic: Amazed of course that any human could glimpse Grace or delude him into believing he glimpsed Grace. Sympathetic to the poor bastard's eventual and inevitable fall from that Grace, deluded or not.

"A fall from Grace, real Grace or imagined, is nothing we, any of us, should ever take the liberty to wish upon any man or woman be they friend or dreaded foe. A human fallen from Grace fails to ever rise to anything else again. Pass the bread and butter would you please, lads?"

The sergeants stared at the dark priest.

He looked at them.

"Don't allow yourselves to be distracted by dichotomy lads."

He slapped his spoon a loud hard crack on the table, "Boys! The bread and butter, if you please."

They jumped and reached for the loaf of bread and the dish of butter and each handed one across the table.

"What one expects and what one perceives and what one gets are rarely the same. Do not fight reality. Human nature is the nature we have. Deluding yourself about human nature is asking for labor that sows nothing but frustration and unwarranted disappointment. Delicious rabbit, do I taste a hint of fennel?"

The priest wiped his spoon with a chunk of bread.

"You do," Laurence told him, "Robert Watson's secret. Not a secret now."

"Robert Watson this is delicious. I failed to spy you sitting there. I apologize. How is your mother? And your sister and the baby?"

Bobby Watson blushed and looked as if he wanted to hide behind Curtis Oliver.

"They are all just fine, Father. Just fine indeed."

"Good, good," Said the hungry priest.

"Baby is not a baby anymore," Bobby Watson answered.

Father Augustus agreed, "No, of course not. This fine lad here must be Curtis Oliver. Am I correct?"

Curtis placed his glass on the table and said, "Yes Father. Quite a day for us all eh, Father?"

"Oh yes, Curtis, oh yes. Quite a day."

They spoke of the quake and the damage reports Donald gathered of Ashbury Heights and the initial impressions of the city engineers and the water company engineers and the rest.

Laurence stood, "Boys, time for us to get back on the

job. Father August, time for you to get on back to your house too."

Everyone stood as the Father was lead to his buggy. A guard was dispatched to return him safely back to his parsonage. Laurence and his sergeants shook hands and slowly returned to their fire line in the other Pritchard buggy.

"Across the bay we go," James said as Donald helped Melinda onto the front seat of the long wagon. Bobby Watson and Curtis Oliver sat in the back with their long shotguns across their laps. Donald and James flanked Melinda on the bench and they too rode down the long hill.

"That Father Augustus scares me," Curtis said, "Any man takes down an officer in the United States Army in two punches and then scoffs at his platoon is either crazy, or I don't know what."

They were silent for a few blocks.

James told them, "Father August is comfortable around Finney and Lucas. He is very comfortable in the McCurren house. He is more friends with Laurence than he is priest. People in public service have images necessary to maintain, so let's say you all saw behind the priest to the man today, this evening. He is very effective. The community loves him, his parish adores him, his bosses promote him, and he's an Auxiliary Bishop now, by the way. I think he spends a lot of time in the middle of people's lives where God is involved too."

Melinda asked, "What do you mean?"

James turned the wagon onto Divisadero Street.

"He sits with the sick. He holds the hands and, sometimes, the souls, of the dying. He assists in the birth of babies. He marries young couples. He talks to the confused and needy, all day long, inside and outside his confessional.

He witnesses a great deal of death. He helps the dying die and he helps the survivors survive. I don't know about you, but I think about religion and God as little as I possibly can.

"I fluctuate between not believing anything at all and quickly praying for as much as I can get for my interests, daily if not hourly. So imagine if you held no doubt about the existence of God. That frees you to do a lot more than ponder the well worn "what if" questions and move on to "what now" actions. Imagine every person knew you only in the context of "what if, God" and "what now, God". Imagine you were the human shape God took in all those lives and for those two starting points. You were the emissary of a being so intricate in some people's lives, wholly despised or ignored in others.

"And you had to bury babies and old people and bless pets and marry people and baptize and give a speech at least once a week. It might get tiring after a few years. The only times I see the Father are for dinner at Laurence and Angela's house or our house. He tells nasty jokes, makes fun of his flock, gets drunk, smokes, and swears. We have a great time. When he gets philosophical or introspective I listen, attentively, because he is the most honest person I have met in my life: the agenda inside him and the agenda he projects are the same. That rarity in him almost makes me believe in God without question or qualification. It makes me believe in him."

Donald asked, "What did he do today? What does a priest do in a disaster?"

"I don't know what other clergy did today but Father August spent the entire day at the fire line saying last rights with the dying and assisting the wounded."

Chapter Twenty Two

They rode to the private pier and the marina landing in silence. Once on the water and in the wind, tacking back across the bay, Donald asked his father, "How was Terry Anne's? Was she open for business?"

James, rolling a loose cigar said, "She was. I saw a judge I'm acquainted with make his way inside. We sat on the wagon and all I could think of was the smell of your Ma and her voice when she said goodbye to me. I had Curtis Oliver ride us away. Went up to Buena Vista Avenue instead. And met you all there at the house."

They stood on the prow silently watching the glow of the disaster and listened to the rumble of explosions, continuing attempts to staunch the spread of the blaze. A toxic steam, more ashes than water, mixed with the spray of the saltwater and the fog from the bay and obscured their view of detail. It continued to coat every surface with black smears and rivulet's of muck.

A spent-looking Old Tim met them at the pier. He led them to the veranda where Finney and he had obviously been working their way through a bottle of whiskey and a bag of fine-cut tobacco. Old Tim excused himself and shuffled off to bed.

"Won't leave me alone. Afraid what my haunted past will do with me on such a night. Morning now," Finney rolled a small cigar as he spoke.

Melinda gave pecks on cheeks and excused herself to bed. Curtis Oliver and Bobby Watson also retired to a guest cottage. The hands on the small yacht made night preparations and soon extinguished the light below decks.

Donald and James each took a small glass from Finney's warming bottle. They stood and watched what he had watched all night. The fog drifted and the drizzle of hellish steam swirled. Through it all was a steady line of small craft making for other shores of the bay.

"I have some fellows around the grounds and watching the waterline with shotguns," Finney spit tobacco crumbs from cracked lips.

To James he said, "Your wife just hit the hay a little while ago."

James raised his eyebrows, "Did she? Maybe I'll follow her. Goodnight, fine sirs."

He placed his glass on the white wooden table at Finney's elbow, flicked his tiny cigar over the railing and entered the dimly lit house.

Inside he climbed the stairs and through the dark tracked the hallway to the door of her usual rooms. His were further down the hall but he stopped and paused. Feeling the engraved brass knob give in his hand, he turned his wrist and pushed the door gently into the silent dark room. His heart beat in his neck and his hands trembled. Fear and excitement to find his wife in warm bedclothes overwhelmed him as he felt his way to the foot of her oversized wooden bed. He heard her breathing and he perceived her body beneath heavy white cotton sheets.

She smelled of soaps, lotions, and sweat. Skirting the bed slowly he knelt and gently kissed his sleeping wife's warm neck.

Donald sat with Finney and rolled another small cigar. He handed it to his old Godfather and rolled another for himself. Silently they watched the far shore.

"If you listen long enough you can hear an occasional scream. Heard a child crying for what felt like the longest time just an hour ago. It stopped abruptly. Thought Tim there was gonna jump in his old skiff and row across to rescue the poor whelp. I never seen anything like this, boy. I feel like I have seen a lot, too. Never anything like this. Sure glad we're over here. We should buy land over here regardless of anything else. What a view, fire or no fire, eh?"

Donald exhaled, "It's awful. You are right, the view of the city before the fire was beautiful. The pristine way the fog drifts in and blankets the entire city is the antithesis to the way the black mass of smoke jumps from the ruins and fills the sky."

They sat in silence and listened.

"Your museum looks fine," Donald eventually said. "No significant damage during the quakes and no fires close by. The electricity still works in that section of the park, don't ask me how. We ate a bite of Welsh rarebit without you. Bobby Watson threw it together earlier today with a coney he shot in the park from your front porch."

"God damn. I love a good rabbit stew. It was good too, huh?"

Finney scowled.

"Oh it was pretty bad. We just ate to be polite."

Donald smiled.

"I am to understand from the obviousness of your lie that it was in fact delicious? One day the only animals in the city parks will be rats, skunks opossum and 'coon. Hope I'm long gone before that happens."

"He shaved fennel from Cook's garden into the mix. It was tasty."

"I ever tell you of the native girl I knew when I was young used to rub a lotion her family made from wild anise on her body? Kaliska was her name. Had a powerful father.

She smeared it on her elbows, heels, and knees before a long walk. She was a big girl and liked to smell good. I always think of her when I eat anything cooked with fennel. First time I lived in the city and tasted licorice I couldn't get enough. She was sassy and, like I say, big.

"When the sun dropped beyond the hills and passed beyond the bay, her thoughts turned to me. Your grandfather Lucas spent a night or two with her too, as I recall. Guess most men she met did. Just the way it was. Woman enjoyed the pleasures of adulthood just as much as men did, back when I was a boy. Never met a man with just one woman in his life until later on when I was older and European and eastern fools started eating California up for themselves.

"Them native women knew things other women I known, Spanish and American, had no idea of. Things easily enough taught. Things easily repeated and mastered over time. I don't know if the ways of physical intimacy were passed down by the women folk. I do know I never met an Indian-hater, Spaniard or American, who ever knew a native physically. If you had, there was no room for anything other than the deepest respect and awe. If for nothing else, the depths of pleasure felt at the hands of a few. Hell I got her likeness made onto a cameo. When I gave it to her, she threw it at me and never let me touch her again.

"Made Lucas laugh because I spent a lot of money and gold getting it carved and mounted. I still have the little scar on my forehead where she hit me with it. It was then Lucas took up with her. She threw that cameo at me and lead him into her shelter while I sat out in the boat we used to sail all around up in the bay. From up near Sam Brannan's claims down all the way to Coyote Creek.

"Kaliska was Miwok. Some the finest folks I ever

know were Miwok. Her Pa was a Ghost Dance prophet and hated when we came round. Even though most the time we were there to apprehend escapees or protect them Miwok from outsiders.

"Kaliska's brother, Yancy, was the one taught me to shoot a gun right and use a knife on another man. Any fool can pick up a revolver and start blasting away, throw a knife, stab at someone. It takes practice and concentration to make a weapon a worthy extension of you. Professionals use tools to complete jobs. Amateurs use the same tools to amuse themselves. Doesn't matter the tool or the trade, professional is always someone to learn from, to watch. Yancy was a strong hunter, probably killed something every week of his life since he was a young boy. Later when the settlers and miners started taking the Miwok land and rights and killing them due to their claims to the land, Yancy started hunting them.

"Never ate them or anything nasty like that. Just assassinated them in small groups. Miwok vigilante. We had a lot of respect for him and covered up his activity more than once. After a time you get a feel for a killer and can tell what he's about by the way he executes a death. Yancy was clean and fast. He mostly stabbed men in the throats. He had strong thoughts about speech and moving through the Great Spirit house without being able to talk was to him, akin to what we think of as hell. Hard to interact with your ancestors and the generations you leave behind if you can't talk because some damn fool Miwok bastard cut your voice out in your sleep.

"Things he taught me, taught us, a person can't read in a damn book. That's one of the problems with you younger farts. Think you can acquire the knowledge of the world from a book. Hell, anyone can sing words from a page of music. Singing well, like building a house or shoeing a horse takes learning. Requires practice, repeated, messed up and corrected.

"I guess if folks didn't have books with instructions on how to do everything and all them big reference annuals and almanacs then the bullies and whiners of the world might starve to death. Other part of learning a trade or a skill from a person who is a master or proficient at their chosen expertise is, the pupil ain't irritating or no one will take them on for instruction.

"Used to be all the simpletons and bullies and whiners a fellow met were dirt farmers because scraping vegetables out of mud took no skill at all. Now they can buy a book, read about how to repair a steam engine and go off and get a job repairing steam engines. But because no one ever showed them how, because the experts they meet cannot stand them, they can be the worst steam engine mechanic in the world. Still, they will sucker someone into giving them a chance. I suppose even a dolt can benefit from experience if they have enough ambition.

"Used to be if you took a horse to get her shoed or a wagon to get a sprung axle replaced you could count on the smith or the carpenter to know their trade. Now a days, with so many manuals and reference books floating about, the smith working on your horse might have the ability to read as his or her only qualification for handling hot metal and your animal's legs.

"I'm not sure, Finney," Donald said. "There's a lot more to know today than there used to be. I have a colleague, Dave Renton. We all call him D.M. He's beginning to build and design fine houses in south California. He and I trade the names of reference books in our letters and many are quite useful. I did learn most of what I know in apprenticeship with builders and contractors. I get a lot of useful knowledge from my reference guides and the sources suggested by my colleagues."

"But you did apprentice. You were, are, likable. Easy to be got along with. So now, you use reference guides to continue in your chosen trade. If you never worked with a master builder or a carpenter and only read the books would you be as good at what you do as you are now?"

"No."

"And if you were an irritating whiner would anyone have taken you on to apprentice?"

"No."

"That is my point."

Finney had the Irish ability to turn any argument around in debate. It was a slight of hand learned as a boy as he listened to his mother and his father's more heated discussions.

Finney continued, "The books I like best these days are these comic books. Some are very funny and smartly executed. Readily available to and understood by the masses. Understood regardless of education and reading ability. Cheap to publish and distribute. What a way to spread complex or even simple ideas. I bet a man could take over another country with the right comic book and complete distribution. Hell, if I was Teddy R. I'd be using a federal mint to manufacture comic books with my programs and proposed legislation outlined in them in simple details.

Donald stared at the rage of the city across the water. They heard the steam getting louder and softer as fireboats concentrated streams on structures to be lost at the waterline.

"You know, there's countless ships buried beneath all that land what's burning," Finney said.

"I remember Lucas mentioned sunken ships before. They foundered and were never recovered?"

"Some did founder. Ship gets so old and rotten there's nothing for it but abandoning her to time. Folks sunk more for one reason or another. As many reasons to sink a man's ship, as there are men. Once on the bottom, getting down to them was risky and thankless. Used to be a bunch of kids ran salvage down at one of the piers. Mostly they were wreck pirates.

"Bunch of ships was sunk just for fill. They'd collect up the old abandoned hulks and use them for battery practice. Sink them and then start filling in with excavated materials right on top of the shells of the ships. More than one of them served as a coffin for some poor bastard. We heard of an entire gang locked into one and sunk a few years back. Don't know if I believe it. The Tanners used to live out on a boat that sunk right out from underneath them. Too bad it didn't take them all down too. It's hard to resist the suck of a sinking ship. But those Tanner boys are right bastards, protected by sin."

Finney fingered the bag of tobacco and pulled the thick wool blanket tighter around him.

Donald took the bag from Finney, removed two pinches of leafy tobacco and slowly began to roll one small cigar at a time. Having worked the fine leaves into a cylinder and tied a bit of string pulled from his shirttail around to hold it together, he handed one to Finney and repeated the maneuver for himself.

"That priest was at the house. He was looking for you. He was irritating. Kept asking me where you were. I did not tell him but Laurence did. I honestly thought he was going to invite himself across. He never did."

"He told the boys from Laurence's brigade "Don't be distracted by dichotomy". Sounds like something Lucas said."

"It was. Lucas loved the Catholic priests. They tracked us down in the wilds, on the bay and lakes, and in the mountains. Lucas cooked for them and drank with them and swapped stories. Admittedly, some were very nice fellows. Many more were just confused youths with no idea what to do with themselves or how to help anyone in the world. Lucas always had a soft place for the confused wanderers of the world. Guess he thought of himself as their champion, if not their patron saint, or honorary league president, priest or no priest.

"Soon he too started seeing them as a distracting presence. They all seemed to be saying, "Look through me to the God that is everywhere and inside you and you have the right to access without interference from other humans. Pay me, pay us, for we are God's keepers and you need a ticket to have a clearer vision of universal order."

"Believe me, most priests and clergy have no clearer idea what God is than a trout has what a tree is."

Donald smiled, "Are we still looking for the Tanner boys?"

Finney picked an old knotty scar on the back of his left hand. He looked to the fog and steam.

"I'm not too sure what's happening with the Tanners. That deputy U.S. Marshal made me so mad on the train. I told him, "Shoot him off the back of the last car above a gulch and I'll pay for a sleeper bunk for you to rest up in to the city". He wouldn't hear of it. Acted as though I was making a joke. Bob Tanner knew I wasn't making a damn joke. Deputy knew I wasn't making a damn joke when he found himself staring at his own weapon held by an angry man whose left arm just got chopped clean off clear up past his elbow.

"I killed Bob Tanner. Then, as luck would have it, Margie killed some more Tanners and their gang on a bridge somewhere along the train line north of Atherton. At the most, there's two Tanners alive. At the least, there's two confused fellows looking for a new bunch of pals to ride with. Margie sure can shoot. She shoots better than I do. Better than any of my other wives. Good quality in a woman. Hell, good quality in a man, too. Anyone can shoot well has an inherent redeeming value. Even if it is a skill rarely called upon. When it's needed, it's really needed.

"You think it's time for coffee? I have some nice freshly roasted berries in a bag in the kitchen."

Donald removed the heavy silver watch from his vest pocket and pushed the small button that opened the intricately inscribed face.

"It's nearly five in the morning. One would never guess from the look of the sky. I suppose this was the first day of an earthquake century."

"I don't know. Quakes come and go. They always make things nuts a while and then we settle back into our little ways. If you boil the water, I'll crush the berries. We can sit here, drink our coffee, and watch the sun cut the haze and murk. Hope the birds decide to sing again today. Cannot recall another day without birdsong. Never seen a sky like that except maybe when the government troops were burning reservations inland. I don't care what anyone says, a fire or explosion is always terrifying and more destructive than anything else."

Donald said, “I suppose so, look at volcanoes. They wipe out entire villages, towns, even islands.”

“That's right,” Finney agreed. “They do indeed. Earthquake starts and stops. Tornado starts and stops. So do tidal waves, hurricanes and mud slides. This fire's been burning for a full day and may burn for another. Or a week. May burn until there is nothing left to burn.”

They sat in silence watching the city.

“Someone should make a comic book about this state. A comic history of California. Not funny, but with the little pictures and the little talk balloons and illustrations with a narrative telling what happened when and where and why. Start with the natives, move on to the Spaniards, digress to statehood and end with our modern days.

“Maybe I'll get some of those fellows who illustrate for the paper to make a comic for me about banking. I'll train all my folks the way I want them trained. Teach them some manners with the comic book too. Illustrate the correct way to talk to a woman. I swear kids these days don't know piss from punch.”

Donald stood, “Come on old man, it's time for coffee and sunrise. Since when do you no longer need sleep?”

“I had a dream before we headed down to Los Angeles. Actually, the dream was on the train to Los Angeles. You know how trains get into your dreams. I had one and in it, I was leaving pieces of my soul along the side of the track as we sped south. I dreamt, the more I slept the more soul I lost, until finally angels talked me into staying with them. Into being one of them, existing with them for the rest of my eternal days. Each held a piece of my soul. Gray pieces. Looked like layers peeled from an onion, thick and juicy, each piece smaller than the one before.

"I started collecting the pieces back from them. They didn't fight me; they were holding them for me. I collected them and put them back together until my soul was intact. I was opening my mouth to ask why my soul flaked off when I woke and heard the train whistle blowing. We were slowing and pulling into some dirt town for water. I haven't slept more than a few naps since. Those are getting shorter too. Funny thing, I don't feel tired. Ever. Mostly I'm jumpy and want to work.

"Can I confess something to you boy? I'm a little grateful this disaster happened when it did. I don't wish anything bad on all the folks who got hurt, killed, and lost loved ones. God knows I do not. All the same, it sure will give us something different to do for a while, right?"

They were in the large kitchen boiling water and cracking roasted coffee berries with a wooden mortar and stone pestle. They crunched and popped.

Donald said, "We never have done anything like this before. For so many people too. The damage is everywhere and no one thing seems to be less important than another is. They may have to bury a few more rotten ships in the bay. We will have plenty of fill to dump on top of their sunken hulls. From what I have seen, we will not be reusing any brick except to fill in sidewalks and piece in damaged paving stones. Building with brick in this city is over. They may not even make good fill. I heard people say the ground near the water was moving like porridge. Hard to imagine. I guess anything can be changed into liquid or a gas when given sufficient external circumstances."

Finney poured the crushed coffee berries into the pot of boiling water and lowered the heat.

"They say that this fir floor and these two coffee

mugs and that hot water are perceived by us to be separate but actually continue and finish one another. Infinitely. That the ability to infinitely see the world we live in, pass though and exist in harmony with, is a skill perfected by, learned, or un-learned, by individuals from the forest. This cup is finite. This coffee-browned, infused hot water is finite. Poured together they are actually the same, just perceived separately.

"This is the kind of thing Kaliska's Pa, the Ghost Dance prophet, used to go on about for hours into the night. Lucas would be in Kaliska's tent and her Pa, the shaman, would be expounding to me, half understanding, completely loaded and facing the wind, about the completeness of the universe. About the totality of existence. Try defending your Anglo background and philosophy to a Miwok. He laughed at me. I was repeating what the missionaries were telling his people for over a hundred years. He could have made my arguments for me. I was a fool and he was a wise old man.

"He used my reverie against me. He cornered me in my own mind and took my boots while I was dumbfounded. Later I learned the tobacco he smoked and shared with me was special and only smoked by the Ghost Dance shaman. He and I smoked a lot of that tobacco together over the years."

They walked back to the veranda and took their same seats. Old Tim sat nearby and Donald rolled some tobacco for him while he got himself a cup of the strong coffee. He muttered in Irish and shuffled back with the coffee and funny cigar to a long white bench that backed the house. He sat and watched the fire, the smoke, the ashes and steam and fog with the two men in silence. Birds were waking, singing their good morning songs, while boats continued to cross the large dark bay. Finney sat and looked at his young friend and the old man from another land who comprehended only what he saw. Finney thought of the women he loved and tear came to his dry old eye.

Life was good, but life was always good. Wives were funny, each one made him laugh. He drained his cup and placed it on the little wooden table. He closed his eyes and slept. Finney McCurren slept a long time.

www.ingramcontent.com/pod-product-compliance
Lightning Source LLC
Chambersburg PA
CBHW020614310726
48979CB00008B/1472/J

* 9 7 8 0 9 8 4 8 9 8 7 0 1 *